Warlord of Ackbarr

Erme Lander

Cover image – Panagiotis Lampridis

ISBN 978-1-8382157-6-7

The events in this book take place about three years after those
in "**Blood Debt**."

Book Four of The Medici Chronicles

More frog than princess, Erme Lander lives in Gloucestershire with her two children and a mad cat.

Other books by Erme Lander

The Vampire –

A Dark Inheritance
A Dark Infection

The Medici Chronicles –

The Lion of Ackbarr
Blood Lore
Medici of Ackbarr
Blood Debt
Warlord of Ackbarr

Lord of Dust

Short stories

Sasha
Willow

Table of Contents

Chapter 1

Mika walked up the cobbled streets of Ackbarr to the keep, the large cat pacing beside her. She raised her hand to greet the people who knew her and nodded to those who knew her more by reputation. She wasn't difficult to spot in the city of darker skinned people, the others who had once made it more cosmopolitan had left several years ago. Those who had stayed had mostly been born here or had nowhere else to go. Even the urchins who'd once gathered on the street corners to add their calls to a noisy marketplace were fewer, everyone had to work hard if they didn't want to starve.

It had only been her reputation that had saved her from many a possible lynching, the last few years hadn't been easy for anyone. Cassai had been blamed and she couldn't help the general populace for believing it. Had it really been three years ago that Petron had left, snarling his revenge? No one could have foreseen what had happened next. The granite city with its many walls and tiers of stone, the defensive cat walks allowing archers to cross from roof to roof without ever touching the ground had been shaken by an enemy it couldn't fight. She clenched her fists within her green robes and knew the people were right, it had been Cassai to hold that dagger to their throats.

"Medici Mikon." The guard at the gates greeted her cheerfully and she stopped to chat to him. She knew he saw what most did, a slim Cassai man with dark blond hair, not the woman she actually was or the shape shifter she could no longer be.

Stafa barely glanced at the guard, moving his head to allow his single eye to peruse the busy courtyard. Mika walked past the now less than pristine walls of the Palace Hospice to enter the huge cavern of the keep itself. She blinked to allow her eyes to adjust from the late autumn sunshine and turned to begin scaling the staircases to the royal apartments. One didn't say no to an official invitation to see Keira and Rufus, even if you were Medici and a friend.

"You didn't have to come though." Stafa ignored her murmured comment and flicked his ears in irritation. The stairs were just at the wrong height for him to climb gracefully, forcing him to bunny hop instead.

This was definitely an official visit, the servant received her courteously into the ante chamber and announced her instead of the normal waving in accorded to friends. The windows were open in the large room, letting in the breeze and Rufus was pacing the floor, chewing on a knuckle. Stafa twitched his whiskers and went to sit in a pool of sunshine. The large warrior swore as he had to avoid the cat who'd sat right in his line of fire.

Mika grinned, it was unlike Rufus to be this distracted. "Problems?"

He grunted, not sharing her amusement. Keira came in and sat down at the table, greeting Mika. She smiled at her husband and patted the chair next to her. He perched on the edge of the table, a hair's breadth away from pacing again.

"What's up?"

Keira said, "We wanted to tell you this before you heard from anyone else."

"We're going to war with Cassai." Rufus said bluntly. "People are going to be watching to see your reactions, you need to know."

Mika sat down slowly on one of the empty chairs. War had been on and off the cards between Ackbarr and Cassai for years since before she'd been born and yet the cracks had always been smoothed until now.

Keira's father had only been able to force a stalemate with the tiny country hidden behind its wall of mountains and thick forests. Unlike other conquered states, Cassai had retained its government, its royal family and many of its officials although as part of an agreement with Ackbarr, it didn't have a standing army.

War between her own country and her adopted one, they were right, now more than ever people would be looking for any sign that she sympathized with her countrymen. She automatically ran her hand through her hair, it had been three years since she'd last bleached it to try and fit in with the expectations of her being a half breed.

The thought of soldiers pouring themselves through the forests of her sparsely populated country was a nightmare that had hung over her for years. The terrain made it ideal for guerrilla warfare and the Cassai army had taken full advantage last time. Mika imagined the small repeater crossbows her countrymen used with the poisoned tips and winced at the number of lives that would be lost.

She managed, "This is necessary?"

Rufus slammed his fist down on the table, "We don't have a choice. Cassai has been thumbing its nose up to Ackbarr for years. We could deal with it then, we can't now. We need to strike."

He was right, the dukes had been howling for blood over the last few years and yet before when her father had been ambassador he'd managed to navigate to keep both sides content if not actually happy. Her half-brother taking over had been the last straw, Koren had known of the difficulties of balancing the two countries and had dealt with it delicately. Petron had no such care.

She bowed her head, “Varian foresaw this.”

“Wish he’d told us,” Rufus snorted.

Keira looked sympathetic, “I’m sorry Mikon, it has to be done.”

She had to deal with this later, she pushed her feelings to one side. Cassai thought her an animal, had threatened her and her friends the last time she’d been there and yet it was the place she’d been brought up, her home. Mika took a deep breath, “You can count on my help, not that I expect I can help much.”

Rufus smiled thinly, “You may be surprised. We’ve been making arrangements for this, for longer than you know. Troops were dispatched to widen the track through the mountains between the border over two years ago, you should go and have a look. We can now get men and horses from one end to the other in three days not ten, and supply carts as well.”

Sensitive to the pressures of court life as a Medici, the last six months had been suspiciously quiet. Mika had wondered what had happened to make them so, the dukes were only happy when either plotting intrigue against each other or war against someone else. Rufus had been scheming both, no wonder the dukes had been kept quiet. Mika remembered the route through the high mountains passes and how they’d all looked the same. “How did you find the way through? Only the guides have all the knowledge and they keep it to themselves.”

“Most men are open to the right persuasion, it was pointed out that as citizens of Fenin they were under Ackbarr jurisdiction and they would be considered traitors for not helping the crown. They have no options for living in Cassai, so why stay loyal to a country who doesn't want them?" He shrugged, "They earnt a decent wage while being guides but we gave them a good reward. Plus some of them were among the first to suffer when all this started. They weren't happy."

"So what have you done? You can't just invade, they'll have men with crossbows looking out for you. They use poisoned arrows, they can fell your outriders in seconds."

"We did some research on what went wrong last time and we've nearly finished the fortress up in the foothills." He paused to allow the fact to sink in, he was right, they'd been busier than she'd known. A proper road through the mountains with a keep at the other end, she was amazed they'd managed to keep it quiet although most people had been simply trying to survive over the last few years. "It's above the treeline so there's no chance of them ambushing us from under cover and I have plans for what's going to happen next but anything else you can remember that will help…"

Rufus had a gleam in his eye, his irritation forgotten. He loved both mischief making and the chance to pit himself against an opponent in battle. His voice softened, he knew the pull she'd feel. "We can't afford to let this go Mika, they have killed our people, decimated the countryside as much as if they put a dagger to our throats."

The echo of her thoughts earlier, "I know, I'll have a think about it. How are you going to stop them finding out about any preparations?"

"That's the fun part, we're not. They know we'll be coming and I want them ready for us." He definitely had a plan.

Keira sighed at her husband's grisly anticipation and said, "We're blocking the ports as well, nothing's going in or out if we can help it."

Mika glanced at her determined face. Keira had shown herself to have a will of steel over the last few years and was more than capable of dealing with many of the dukes. "Cassai is completely isolated then?" She thought there'd been less product from her country around although she'd assumed that was because of the decline in popularity.

"Yes. There's no way through the pass without us knowing and it'll be difficult to get out by sea. They aren't welcome in any ports anyway."

"There are other ways through the mountains," Mika mused. However there was no way any Cassai could sneak into the country, they were too obvious amongst the shorter, duskier skinned people of Ackbarr.

Kiera asked, "Do they use them?"

"No, they don't like them."

"That's strange, I wonder why, most countries would be looking for different ways through. Are you sure on that?"

"Yes." Mika wasn't sure if she ought to mention the Cassin and their shape changing ability. She was fairly certain Tamar hadn't talked much about Selene when they'd come back. Rufus had thought she was a peasant girl at Tatton and had openly teased him about her, not noticing his younger brother's uncharacteristic quietness.

She wondered how her family was, whether her mother had ever changed back, and what would happen to her little sisters if they were caught. She didn't even know where they were living, she hadn't seen them since she'd been fifteen. Mika closed her eyes, Ackbarr hadn't had any such mercy from Cassai. There were little sisters here who'd died too, she had to stay focussed. She opened her eyes to see Keira lay a hand on Rufus' wrist and he closed his mouth on the words he had been about to say.

Keira said, “I’m determined to deal with this. Ackbarr never got as far as Dubari last time, this time will be different. We will do this with as few casualties as possible.”

Mika believed her. “But there will be some.”

“Yes.”

War, more death and dying only this time it would be a deliberate hacking apart of those she cared about. There would be no hiding from it. Her friends had been brought up to wage war, consider battles and kill. Mika shuddered, even the cat only killed what it needed to and pushed away the thought of irresistibly small furry creatures that went squeak and ran – that was different.

“I’ll have a think.” She bowed to her rulers and clicked her fingers at Stafa who pulled himself away from the sunlight with a groan.

Chapter 2

Mika walked out of the gates, even here the countryside had changed in the last three years. The copses dotting the fields had grown, new saplings taking over adjacent fields. The settlements close to the river had expanded in places and houses had been allowed to fall down in others.

It didn't matter, she was only here for one thing. Tucking her backpack into a bush, she looked down at Stafa and took a deep breath. The night was young, the smaller of the two moons was up and the other would be appearing shortly. Stafa shivered, a soft encouraging purr bursting from him. Relax, let it out. She stood with her shoulders dropped and allowed the cat to take over. It slid around her mind, sinking into her body. Her partial change made her look grotesque, neither cat nor human, a nightmare. It was the worst of both worlds and it was all she had left.

Once a week or so, she'd come out here and let the cat out, even when she was exhausted. It was the only way to deal with it otherwise it took over while she slept and she couldn't cope with the lack of control. Waking up to find herself in bed with Nim several years ago had been the last straw, she knew it couldn't do any damage out here.

The cat whispered its joy of the night to her. Never mind the fact that it only had two legs instead of four and that her senses were pitiful in comparison to what they had been when she could change fully. It stretched her body and bent to bump noses with Stafa. Leave the human world to its intrigue and politics, the cat didn't care for such things. Even the relentless mending of people would be supplanted by monochrome and the vivid splash of heart's blood.

Her slender shadow stretched out in front of her, the night was quiet apart from the soft rustle of leaves and the abomination she was, scanned the landscape. All senses on high alert, lifting her head to scent the breeze, she spotted something moving. Stafa saw her freeze and crept sideways, ears rotating, his single eye flicking. Mika allowed herself to sink into a sleep while the cat took over, she had no wish to see what they'd do to the rabbit. For some reason when she'd actually changed her shape, it hadn't bothered her as much. The thought of her own body toying with a smaller creature for sheer joy made her feel ill.

She woke much later with the cat sated on the night and her face stiff with blood. Mika pulled herself up to wash in a nearby stream. Both moons were nearly full, their reflected light bringing the countryside into a sharp black and white focus.

The cold water brought her back to reality. War, she'd not been able to get the concept out of her mind all day and she knew her distraction had been noticed. Who could she be loyal to? The country she'd been brought up in didn't want her and yet the thought of soldiers pouring out of the mountains… Rufus was an able commander, his quicksilver mind capable of changing direction to complement the way the battle moved, she had no doubt he would get further than Keira's father.

Ackbarr had been her home for nearly twenty years, she loved the people and walking the cobbled streets in the forbidding city and the Medici had accepted her as one of their own. The Medici – they would debate supporting the invasion shortly. She dropped her head and decided she would go with their decision.

Mika slumped at the table in her rooms having finished her teaching for the morning. Normal life for the Medici had only resumed in the last six months or so and even then the gaps in the classes were desperately obvious. It would take years to fill the shortfall, to send out replacements into the countryside healing and collecting information. She yawned, her body didn't get the rest it needed while the cat was running around with it.

It had been three years since the sleeping sickness had first raised its head during the autumn. The first inkling outside the ports had been an unknown person joining the harvest exodus, walking from village to town to village and spreading the illness before people realised. While there was a simple enough cure, it spread far and fast before symptoms appeared. Before they knew it, the crops were rotting in the fields and people had fled panicking and infecting others.

She knew of the sickness from Lin's journals. It started as a simple tiredness, leading to a coma like sleep and then the body turning on itself to rot while the patient lay helpless. She'd read about Lin's experiences when it had swept through Ackbarr the first time. His wife had died of it, leading to his travelling to Cassai and meeting her parents. That in turn had been the catalyst for him to take her on when he'd found her starving in the woods.

It had been planned well, and it had been planned. This hadn't been a normal outbreak, it had been brought not only to the ports but also across the mountains to the fields of Fenin – the breadbasket of Ackbarr. While the illness was known of and there tended to be small pockets of it close to the ports, they hadn't been ready for it cropping up everywhere. Most people in the countryside hadn't the knowledge of it and weren't immune. Fewer still had any idea of how to treat it and getting the correct medicine out to people had been almost impossible. Peddlers and quacks had sold their own cures and disappeared into the night, not waiting to see the inevitable results. Riots and rumours had abounded.

It had been tough for both Keira and Rufus' rule when the harvest had failed to be brought in that year. There was little in the storehouses for winter and less for the normal spring lean time, hitting the countryside hard and the cities harder. There was famine, those who had nothing tramping along the roads and lords complaining of others stealing their workers while poaching any they could find. It had taken three years to recover, to start the sowing and harvesting everyone depended on.

Mika had worked tirelessly, as had all the Medici despite some falling prey to the sickness and yet more becoming ill from sickness brought on by exhaustion. She mourned for the knowledge lost as much as the lives. Varian had died at the beginning of the outbreak, at least he'd had a proper funeral, so many others had been thrown in pits to be covered in lime. Even Lord Eldon himself had succumbed, death hadn't flinched at meeting that hawk eyed gaze and taking what was due.

Her own immunity had been a mixed blessing considering her heritage. She'd been aware of the looks while she treated people, knowing that she'd had it as a young child. A simple illness in Cassai, it was rarely fatal. In fact it was usual to treat for it the minute a child looked to be under the weather. So many deaths for such a simple illness in another country. The information that it was normal in Cassai spread almost as quickly as the disease and it meant her country was disliked more than ever.

It was widely agreed that the sickness had been Cassai's revenge for the removal of their ambassador. Shortly after Mika had come back from the mountains, Keira had thrown Petron out of Ackbarr after refusing to agree to his demands. Petron had barely escaped with his life when Keira's displeasure had become common knowledge. Those in Ackbarr had become surprisingly fond of their slender ruler considering the patriarchal mindset.

Mika's fingers dropped to touch the soft ruff of the cat sitting next to her. There'd been a few times when his presence had stopped a crowd turning into a mob. It was just as well she had decided to give up the idea of becoming Court Medici. She'd not mentioned her reasons why to Rufus and it had been one of the few times he'd been frustrated with her.

Every time she failed to remember something her heart would stop, wondering if this was the beginning of her decline. She'd firmly tuck it to one side, the fear of degenerating was no way to live and yet it loomed over her. She made her forgetfulness into a joke while she taught, using it to hone the bright minds in front of her.

Mika reminded herself that the organisation who'd taken her in also protected her, they would make sure she was safe if she degenerated to the point of not being able to look after herself. They'd accepted her excuses that she could no longer deal with surgery without comment and employed her elsewhere. It wasn't the smell or sight of blood, it was the sweetroot used to anesthetise the patients. Her body craved the smell and it made her hands shake. The fact that she'd been addicted to it simply served as a warning to others.

A soft knock interrupted her thoughts and she pulled herself upright.

"Medici?" Rosita poked her head around the door.

"You have a problem Rosita?"

The girl nodded and slid inside. "I was looking for Jon, it's the abattoir, they're refusing to take me."

Jon had nearly succumbed a year ago and she'd treated him herself, desperate for him not to die. She hadn't realised up to that point what a fixture he'd been in her life. She'd vowed to take a leaf out of the cat's book at that point – one day at a time and to enjoy what she had. He'd moved into her apartment from then onwards, not caring what was said of two men sharing.

"Because you're a girl?"

She squirmed, "They say it's not for ladies and I'm not strong enough. They don't want me fainting and having to be responsible for me but Jon said I have to go to get the experience."

"That's correct, it's a rite of passage in some ways. You'll be able to deal with anything after you've worked there for a week." Mika snorted, "I think some of those men forget how many farm women deal with wringing chicken necks and everything else at butchering time. Not for ladies indeed. Have you got those split skirts I suggested you get?"

Rosita was looking white and nodded, "Mother doesn't agree with them, I had to hide them from her."

Mika was merciless, "Go and put them on, add a linen shirt and I'll find you a boy's leather tunic to go over the top. Make sure your hair is tied back securely and won't fall in your face."

"Are you sending me back?"

"I'm doing better than that." She smiled tightly, "I'm going with you."

Mika got dressed for the abattoir, musing that the sickness had forced more changes to happen faster, the Medici had been forced to take on girls.

Rosita still took the strain of being the oldest and anything new was normally a battle however her obvious brightness helped. The priestesses of Temple Library being more prominent during the last few years, sometimes travelling miles with their female guards had also brought a wider acknowledgment of women's capabilities. She wondered if Lissina's old guard Dabora was still alive and shook her head, that was one rat cage she didn't want to unlock. Dabora had not been sure about her, having lived with woman who healed and were warriors, Mika's deception of being a man wasn't hugely strong around her. She'd appeared to accept Lissina's explanation but Mika couldn't risk being uncovered.

The foreman was adamant when Mika took Rosita back that they couldn't have her in the building. Rosita was looking small and boyish in her split skirts and tunic. He waved his hand at her, pointing out they didn't have the man power to cosset her. Rosita was nearly in tears, boys she could face down but this man was a huge ex-soldier, his face scarred and seamed from long service.

Mika had worn her Medici robes, a reminder of her status and the agreement they had with the abattoir. She'd not taught Rosita and passed her on to be sponsored by Jon to have her career stymied by this. "Foreman, this journeyman has helped through the sickness as much as any of the boys." She emphasized the 'journeyman', Rosita hadn't been spared anything much to her mother's loud distress.

"That's not the point." He was looking stubborn. "She's half the size of anyone else here, I'm not picking her up every time she gets trampled."

"Fine." The foreman looked shocked as Mika shucked her robes and slung them on the back of a rail, standing in her own leather tunic and trousers. "Looks like I'll have to teach her then." She faced him down, "Which chute is free?" His eyes narrowed and Mika knew they'd get sent every large and difficult animal until Rosita fell over from tiredness. He indicated a chute at the far side and all the men turned to watch as Rosita picked her way through the muck. Mika swore under her breath and took Rosita's arm.

"What?" she asked.

"See that shit?" Mika pointed at a pile. Rosita winced at Mika's language and nodded. "Go stand in it."

Rosita raised her skirts, showing her tidy boots. A derisive laugh from one of the men and her eyes filled with tears. Mika held her gaze, Rosita took a deep breath and stomped over. A heavy scraper was propped against the wall next to it. She picked it up and swung it at the pile, flinging manure in the direction of the joker. His laugh cut off into a volley of swear words as the dung hit him. Rosita tidily propped the scraper up again and walked back to Mika, ignoring the language coming not just from her target but also the laughter from his work colleagues.

"Where do we start Medici?" Her face was still white and her lips compressed but she'd been in other situations just as bad despite being a seventeen year old girl.

"I think you've already got off to a good start journeyman, this way." Mika raised her voice, "Stev? I'd like a sheep through our chute first please."

Rosita scrambled on top of the rails as the sheep came hurtling through, crazed by the noise both inside and out. Mika talked her through what she'd have to do and saw the hammer was far too heavy. She could see Rosita panicking, they'd have to get this over with quickly. "I'll help you, we'll sort this one and take it over for skinning."

It would be easier to deal with all the shocks at once, she was aware of the men watching while they worked. Mika reached around to help Rosita grasp the hammer, wrapping her fingers around hers. She narrowed her eyes, waiting for the right moment and snapped an arm out to grasp the sheep. Using herself as a pivot she pulled Rosita round to crack the hammer against its skull. Rosita stared as it fell to the floor.

"Here, it's been knocked out. There's the pulley, you'll need to throw the rope over and attach its feet together using this knot." She pulled the unconscious animal up and through the gate easily, tying the rope to keep it suspended above a large barrel.

She offered Rosita her knife. "Stand out of the way and pull the head back." At the girl's hesitation she said, "You cut here." Mika took hold of both of Rosita's hands again, her touch professional and swept the knife across, the skin parting with a single slash and felt how Rosita cringed away. "Look, can you see how the arteries have been severed?"

Mika kept her voice light and dispassionate, at some point soon Rosita would be invited to surgery. She'd done all the theory but she had to be ready for the brutalities of their trade. Mika had had the cat to help her deal with this, Rosita had nothing. The girl kept her head down, hiding the tears in her eyes but Mika could see the determined look on her small face. She dragged the dead sheep across the building to the flensing area using the pulley and started cutting and tugging the hide of the body as she was shown, her clothes quickly becoming red with blood.

Rosita stopped, breathing heavily as she pulled the hide off and another man came over to claim it. He nodded to her, a grudging respect in his eyes. Rosita blinked as the man came back, expecting him to sneer.

Instead he held out another hammer, "Try this lady, it's lighter."

Rosita held out both hands to take it. "Thank you. We go back to the chute Medici?" Her voice was small. Mika hid a smile, Rosita would show them she could deal with this, she just needed a chance.

Mika sat in her bath aching that night and knowing Rosita would be feeling worse. She'd made Rosita bath in her apartments before she'd gone home, her mother would've had hysterics at her daughter looking like a slaughterman. The girl had done well and Mika had given her the grudging praise she'd expected.

She smiled, after the first man offering the hammer only small animals had been sent through the chute. Other men had come across to help, showing Rosita the how's and why's and even the foreman had given his grudging acknowledgment that her journeyman could do the brutal job without fainting. Tomorrow she would be learning how to dissect the animals and Mika reckoned she wouldn't need to supervise all day. The cat had sulked at the noise and amount of death, she sank lower into her bath, she felt the same.

Mika rubbed her face, once Rosita had proved she could deal with blood and gore the next difficulty would be surgery. Half her problem was the strength needed to do a lot of these things and she'd heard mutterings about Rosita only doing the work considered suitable for a girl. Stuff that, she knew Rosita had the intelligence to do all aspects and the determination. She knew herself that half of the solution was technique and that was something she could teach better than any man.

While they didn't always get on, the last few years had been easier with teaching the girl and Rosita now appeared to accept Mika driving her to produce her best.

The noise of her clothes being pushed along the floor roused her from her thoughts. Stafa was sniffing and rolling over them, enjoying the scent of blood and gore. Mika sat up and swore. "Stafa, leave them alone!"

The large cat narrowed his eye and flicked his ears back as she threw a handful of water at him - time to get out.

Chapter 3

Mika walked into the library where the Medici meetings were held. The room was a haven of quiet, the books inviting you to lower your voice. Most people were there already. There weren't many, like in many professions their numbers had been depleted from the sleeping sickness.

They'd held back the rioting people desperate for cures with the help of the city guard. She couldn't blame the common people, watching loved ones being consumed from within while sleeping wasn't pleasant. It hadn't any other symptoms, just the tiredness leading into coma. It had left people terrified of sleeping and refusing to sleep weakened the body further meaning they were more likely to catch it.

She shivered, the main problem had been keeping supplies of the medicine. Certain plants had been decimated close to centres of populations. Luckily some of those plants grew like weeds, the Medici had farmed them with military precision and checked those going in and out to make sure they weren't hiding any.

The soft murmur of conversation soothed her with the smell of dust and books. The hours she had spent in this place, looking for some obscure reference made by Varian and in the knowledge that he would expect her to find it and verify if it was still correct. Joy sparked through her at the thought of sinking into the words of Medici written decades before her birth and then wrestling to find out if the information was still correct. It had kept her alive in the most human meaning of the word. Varian's presence, the fact that he wouldn't accept any less than the best had also helped keep the inevitable decline of the beast away from her.

Jon smiled as she made her way towards him. At most they'd had the odd raised eyebrow at their living together, very few knew of her concealed sex however the last few years had done more for breaking down prejudices than anything else. Girls were now a commonplace sight in the apprentice ranks of both Medici and other occupations, there was little space for complaints. She'd caught Rosita dispensing advice on more than one occasion to a worried girl and noticed they banded together. As a result, the boys were also upping their game, not wanting to be outdone. She smiled, a bit of healthy competition was never bad. The room was called to attention by the Medici at the lectern and she turned with everyone to listen.

The debate and voting were swifter than she'd thought it would be and there was very little in the information given that she didn't already know. The debate was important considering the dukes would be unlikely to go to war without medical help. On this occasion, it was acknowledged that war would happen whether they liked it or not and the support given by the Medici would help alleviate any further suffering.

Mika controlled her despair and spoke to a few colleagues before walking swiftly out, knowing that even the Medici would be watching to see her reactions. The sunlit morning felt different - it was happening. The Medici in supporting Keira had removed the last barrier. They had voted not to support campaigns before, stopping them in their tracks and forcing those responsible to find other means.

She had abstained in the vote to begin with, watching the flurry of hands being raised for the affirmative vote. A few voted for no, their views would be respected and they would be found other duties not connected. The Medici at the lectern had asked if anyone wish to change a vote and she had raised her hand. Her voice had been steady, belying her stomach as she told them that while she couldn't condone the war, she would go with the majority vote and help with the effort.

Thinking she needed to get some air, she walked outside to the curtain wall where she and Jon used to sit when younger. The marketplaces and streets buzzed, the normality feeling strange with her new knowledge of what was going to happen. Mika had always voted no before, the same as Lin had. Her feelings were that she was a Medici - a healer not a warrior and they shouldn't support any invasions.

The view didn't help as much as she thought it might, it merely showed the devastation the sickness had brought in full. Parts of the plains were growing wild, previously thriving settlements abandoned. She'd even heard that the slums she'd ridden through at Fenin had been razed in efforts to contain the contagion. So much destroyed by what was a simple childhood illness in Cassai. There was no way she could stay here and wait for news, she was going to have to go to war with Rufus.

Mika turned away from the plains and climbed the steep paths back to the Medici building, not paying attention to anything. Her anxiety wasn't helped by the cat inside her being bored and uninterested in her worries about another human generated slaughterhouse. Having seen the plains, it whispered to go out there and forget. It had grown with her, it was no longer a wild being separate from herself. If it chose to, it could take her body over and interact with others with few the wiser. They'd both lost out by her taking those drugs to suppress it.

The Medici building loomed above her and she smiled. Its very solidity reminded her of what she was, the training and determination she'd had to get to where she stood now within the organisation. She'd had chances and opportunities to do things she'd never thought possible due to them, she'd not shy away from this challenge either.

Stafa was sprawled on her bed when she got back. Mika sat next to him, her eyes far away, and stroked his thick fur until he groaned in pleasure. What did Rufus have in mind? How could he get through the hidden bowmen without losing half his army, even with a road wide enough for carts through the mountains. It was too easy to imagine the soldiers pouring through her parent's compound, the sanctuary of her childhood and trampling the gardens…

She stopped as the door opened and Jon came in. He sat on the bed behind her and pulled her back against him.

"How you doing?"

She shrugged, "Everyone's watching to see how I'll react, it's not pleasant."

"Ignore everyone else, they don't like it either." Jon persisted, "How are you?"

Mika looked down at the cat stretched out beside her and rubbed the soft ball behind his ear. "I'm going to have to help Ackbarr invade my country, I can't stay separate from this. If I can stop people getting hurt, people dying then it will be worth it."

"And the people you know there?"

"I don't actually know that many now and I rarely left the compound when I was a child." Still, there was her childhood friend – Alma. Where was she now? What about her little sisters, would she even recognise them if she saw them? Jon's arms tightened and a trickle of warmth curled like an ink drop in water across her mind.

"What about your family?" He had a way of asking the difficult questions she wanted to avoid.

"Mama disappeared the night the twins left, I don't know if they found her." She sighed, "If Jehanne was correct then she may well have stayed in that form if there wasn't anything left to hold her human. With Koren, I've no idea. I've not heard anything since Petron took over. My little sisters were married the last I heard, both with children."

"You also have family in the stronghold, ones you know nothing about."

"I know enough to know they won't care about me." With the bitterness, she noticed the warmth spreading out across her mind, puddling into a lust filled pool. "Stafa, no. Fuck off."

"Is he…?" Jon queried.

"He keeps trying and to be honest, since I stopped the drugs he's turned into a bit of a sex pest. You'd never guess he's had his balls chopped off."

Jon winced and peered around her to say, "You can have her when she's in the same shape as you. This shape – she's mine." He pulled Mika away from the cat. Stafa sneezed and looked away.

"Jon, you know I can't change."

He snickered, "Of course, why do you think I'm so relaxed about it?" He kissed her and she pulled away, laughing.

"I'm going to ask Rufus if I can go with him."

Jon nodded, "I thought you might. You can't be responsible for the whole country you know."

"If I can help just a little…"

"I'll be coming with you." He sounded determined.

"People die in these things Jon." The feeling of his arms around her was a security she didn't want to lose. His becoming ill had highlighted her dependency on him and the terror of losing him. It made her uncomfortable at times.

"No shit." She wriggled, he was making fun of her. "I know what you mean but I'm still coming."

"You hate this too."

"Yes but I'm not letting you go on your own." Jon kissed the side of her head firmly and she gripped his hand in the appreciation she couldn't express.

"I need to see Rufus."

It took a day or so, even with her status as Medici and a friend one did not simply drop in on Keira and Rufus.

"I just wanted to say that with the Medici's decision to support you, I'll give any help I can but I want to go to Cassai with you."

Keira's face lit up and she held out a hand, "I know this is hard for you Mika, I wouldn't have blamed you for wanting to stay out of it."

"I can't." Mika gripped her hand briefly and dropped it. It had been tougher than she'd thought to ask this much.

There was a hard respect in Rufus' face. "Good, I may have a place for you in my plans." He narrowed his eyes and asked, "What do you know about a Cassai named Aurin?" The suddenness made her jump, Aurin had been the last thing she'd thought they'd ask about.

"The Aurin I know is a spy for the Cassai government, he also works for the Cassin."

"Cassin?" Rufus had a sharp look on his face.

“The people in the mountains I visited a few years ago.” She took a deep breath, apart from Varian she’d not mentioned this to anyone. “They’re changers.”

He demanded, “More secrets Mika?”

“What do you mean?” Keira was looking confused.

Mika hadn’t exactly kept it from her but it wasn’t the sort of thing she tended to talk about. She explained, “Some of the royal family in Cassai can change into cats, it’s not a sought after habit, we’re regarded as animals and exterminated if found.”

“We? You can change yourself into another shape?”

Mika knew what was going to be asked and tried to head it off by saying, “Do you remember me smoking sweetroot? That was me making an effort to subdue it, it didn’t work.” She forced the next sentence out, “The same happened to my father, Jace.”

Keira shuddered. “I remember Jace, he frightened me as a child. I didn’t realise he was your father.” Her hand went over her mouth, “You were rumoured to have killed him…”

“Yes. I did.” Her curt tone cut off any further questions about her biological father. She couldn’t talk about why, that was too close even with all the years in between.

“Can you show me?” The inevitable question and Rufus smiled tightly, he’d never seen her in her other form and Jon and Tamar had spread the lie that she wasn’t trustworthy around the few others who knew she could change.

“No, I’ve crippled my ability by using drugs to try and control it. They weren’t working and I came off my addiction to them when I visited the Cassin.”

She didn't want to show anyone the monstrosity she'd become, she'd not even shown Jon.

Keira's eyes were full of sympathy as Rufus went back to the point bugging him, "So why didn't you or Tamar tell me about these Cassin?"

"I didn't think you needed to know about them and they are hardly a threat to Ackbarr Rufus."

"They're Cassai and in our mountains."

They're not wanted by Cassai, and it's not exactly Ackbarr's territory either." Her voice softened, "They're dying."

"What do you mean?"

Mika explained, "They were used by Cassai as animals for years, they escaped when your father invaded the last time. The Cassai keep a line of fires across certain areas where the mountains touch the forest. They smoke herbs on them to repel them. Tamar, Jon and I stumbled across that line when we were escaping years ago. It's very effective and the Cassin rarely come down to the forestland. Only some of them have realised that they're not living very long due to what they are. They have no history, no way of keeping any knowledge going."

Rufus looked at her sharply, "They don't live long and they're changers? Does this impact on you too?"

"Yes." She kept her face still, trust Rufus to pick up on that. "At some point the cat will take over and I won't be fully human anymore."

"Fuck."

She managed a slightly sick smile, "Something like that, yes."

"When?"

"Any time from now onwards. Jon and I are working out how to deal with it." A lie, neither of them had a clue.

He huffed, his eyes blank while he thought. Eventually he said, "If you need anything, talk to me."

"Either of us, Mika," Keira said softly.

Mika bowed her head, "I spoke to Varian when I came back from the mountains, I recorded everything I learnt, do you want it?" She was opening up her life to them, she had to trust and prove she was trustworthy.

"That would be useful." Rufus motioned sharply, indicating he wanted to change the subject. He asked, "That community you found, would they help the Cassai?"

"No, they hate them."

"Would they help us? If they look like Cassai then we could use them."

"I don't know, it depends who's in charge now. Jehanne was older than me. What was this about Aurin?"

"We've had rumours of Cassai spies on the borders, in particular about this man. Is there any way he could get this far on his own?"

"No. There's no way he could get here, he looks too Cassai. He'd get ripped apart." Never Cassai in his own lands, always everywhere else. Mika wondered if there were many other half-breeds who'd struggled outside the Cassai borders in the last three years.

Keira said, "Apparently he's been seen close to Tatton. You know what he looks like, we want you over there to find him and bring him back under guard."

"Tamar's met him as well."

"Tamar stays away from him. Ignacio will go with you, I'm trusting you both to get him here in one piece." Rufus was taking no chances, Tamar had value as a hostage. "Let me have those notes of yours and I'll decide what to do."

Chapter 4

Tatton was curiously quiet, all the workers gone from their fields. Lissina had written at infrequent intervals during the last three years and Mika had been touched by the way she'd described her marriage to Maksim, they appeared to have found a gentle love together. She could imagine the sombre Medici adoring her friend and from the sounds of it, he indulged her completely.

None of her letters had described the sickness as being bad. Living at the back end of beyond, Maksim had found it a simple task to close his land off to strangers with the single road in and out. Mika missed Lissina, they'd been part of each other's lives for so long and letters didn't fill the gap. All her friends who knew her secret were spread out now and they'd had so little opportunity to meet up with other responsibilities.

Mika indicated to Ignacio which way to go to the keep and they clattered through the marketplace. Again, it was unusually quiet, all of the shop fronts locked shut and none of the merchants touting for business.

It had been a hard ride, Rufus had given her a small party of soldiers as well as Ignacio for protection. She'd worn her Medici robes with a hood over her face to cover her features and paler hair and had her rapier by her side. She was a target for those in the countryside who didn't know her. The soldiers ordered food and she ate in her room every night in the few inns that they used. She had a wariness she'd not had since she'd left Fenin so many years ago.

Jon hadn't been happy to be left in Ackbarr despite knowing he had to keep up his own duties.

He'd just hugged her and left to go to the hospice. Stafa had glowered and raked her bedclothes into a more convenient pile for him to sleep on. Jon would let him out for exercise and feed him if he wasn't able to hunt in the countryside. They had a quiet truce these days if Mika wasn't around, Stafa had been surprisingly adaptable, ignoring the humans edging around him in his day to day life. It had made her wonder more about his origins and knew she'd never find out.

They found the workers and the townsfolk in a mob outside the keep entrance, the guards keeping them at bay. Mika flicked her Medici hood over her face, as a mob they wouldn't care that she'd treated them years ago and she had no wish for her actual sex to be discovered by accident either.

She flinched at the cries of "Get the Cassai," and her own soldiers drew close around her. Ignacio moved forward to deal with the situation. They forced their way through the mob, joining with the keep guards and Mika could see the relief on their faces at the unexpected help. She kept her hood up as she dismounted and kept it up until she'd shut the door to the hall.

Mika pulled it down in relief and Maksim's steward rushed over to greet her, "Medici Mikon, thank goodness. Someone from the city at last"

"Rufus sent me. Why are people out there?"

"Didn't you get the message? We sent it by the fastest means possible." At her look, he continued, "One of the guards heard the workers yelling just over a week ago. They'd caught a Cassai and they were busy beating him up. Our guards only just managed to get him out alive."

"Caught someone?" She felt for whoever they'd caught, it didn't matter who they were.

"He's dyed his skin and hair to pass enough from a distance, he must have been planning to travel further. Lord Maksim and the journeyman have been looking after him, he's not able to move yet. It doesn't matter what we do, there's been a mob out there ever since despite the overseer trying to get them to work. We sent a message to Ackbarr to find out what to do with him."

"Okay, let me have a look. Where is he?"

"He's in the practise room." The steward indicated the stairs and Mika strode up, hearing her own soldiers coming into the hall. She absently kissed Lissina as they passed, to upset to notice much more than Lissina had filled out over the last three years.

The practise room was shuttered, a long form lay on the bed, one arm raised up and shackled to the bed post. The other was swathed in bandages across his chest and the face had been dressed as well. Mika winced at the snuffle coming out as he breathed softly. She found herself tensing and was unsure why and then noticed the familiar seductive smell of the sweetroot that must have been used to sedate him.

She had to concentrate, her fingers already wanting to dip into the non-existent pouch for her rolls, go through the motions of lighting it and feel the warmth of the smoke in her lungs… Mika clenched her teeth, pinching her arm to get her brain to see what was in front of her. She'd not done surgery for the last three years for this very reason, she couldn't be trusted around the stuff. All that training wasted… She stood, breathing shallowly - not wasted - she still taught the techniques needed and she could vouch for the addictive qualities of the drug for any students tempted to mess with it.

The door opened quietly behind her and she turned to see Tamar limp in. He beckoned her into the next room where the supplies were kept and closed the door behind them. Mika walked over to the window and pulled it open, breathing deeply.

"Mikon, I'm so pleased to see you." He sounded relieved, "We didn't know what else to do."

"I didn't get the message, I've come on your brother's business. I need to travel to the Cassin stronghold."

Tamar choked out a laugh, "Well we've got the best person to help you, although he's not in a fit state to take you there."

"What do you mean?"

"Didn't you recognise him?" His face turned concerned as she stared. "That's Aurin on the bed."

Her jaw dropped, "I was asked to look into finding him, there's been rumours spreading from somewhere about him being on the border. He shouldn't have got caught, he's too good for that."

"We still don't know entirely how it happened, he's not regained consciousness properly yet. His horse was wandering around terrorising everyone, it took a mare on heat to bring him in. Nobody dares go near the bastard." She remembered the ugly brown horse and Aurin telling Selene that it was battle trained. Tamar continued, "I had to operate on his arm, I think he'll get most of the use back."

Most of the use, she felt sick. Maksim had been a pioneering Medici at surgery, Tamar's work would have been good. "I'll take a look at him."

He nodded and hesitated, "Lissina will be pleased to see you as well."

Mika dismissed the comment with a wave of her hand. Lissina was a friend and she'd not seen her in years but she had to check on Aurin and then think about how to get through the mountains. "I'll have a chat with her later."

"It's important Mikon, didn't she tell you?"

“What?”

Tamar twisted, stretching out his foot, “It’s not confirmed officially but she’s pregnant. She was talking about writing to you.”

Mika’s mouth fell open. She’d had the occasional letter from Lissina and known how much she and Maksim liked each other but this was wonderful. Lissina had never thought she could become pregnant after Jace’s attack and hadn’t wanted to try. Mika blinked back tears, conscious of Aurin in the next room and managed, “That’s wonderful news Tamar.”

He chuckled, “Thought you’d want to know just don’t tell her I told you.”

“She’d never believe me the amount you talk…”

“I’ll leave you to check on Aurin, I know you’ll want too.” No insult to his or Maksim’s skills, he knew what Aurin had meant to her. “Open the windows if the smell’s too strong.” He smiled and limped out of the room.

Mika opened the sick room shutters slightly to let some daylight in and the smell of sweetroot out. Aurin’s hair had been dyed dark enough to get away with looking like a man from Fenin and she could see how he’d shaded his skin to match, making the most of his wider cheekbones. Close up it didn’t quite work.

Tamar had only cleaned off enough to see to his wounds, she took a bowl of water and a soft rag and began cleaning the rest of his face. There were more bruises under the darkened skin. He was a mess, as well as the wound to his face, both his eyes had been blackened and his nose broken. He was a good fighter but it must have been a mob. She shuddered at the thought of being trapped in a crowd of hands, hitting and pulling with no care for the human life inside its fragile casing. She just couldn't understand why he'd allowed it to happen. He stirred under her hands and she shushed him.

Aurin's mouth moved and she trickled a tiny amount of water into his mouth until he stopped swallowing and it ran down the side. He sighed, the only sound he'd made apart from the breath whistling. Checking the rest of him, she found his ribs well wrapped and other bruises marking his body. A long rope burn sliced across his neck, he'd been lucky they hadn't had any weapons.

Mika found tears filling her eyes and wiped them away with a shaking hand. This form lying on the bed wasn't the Aurin she remembered. The light on his hair, both bleached and its natural shade of bronze, the gleam in his long eyes and the feel of his body against hers. He had always sparked something other than the warm companionship she had with Jon, not that she'd ever wanted to acknowledge it once she and Jon had got together. He was the part of her that was Cassai and another being that had been hurt by her home country. She brushed his hair away from his face and left.

Mika caught a servant and asked for her room, not wanting to face anyone for the moment. Her bags had been placed on the bed and she shifted them across, missing the warmth and smell of cat. She'd had her orders to find a way through the mountains to the Cassin stronghold if Aurin wasn't around, they wanted her to speak to Jehanne and find out if she was still in one piece mentally. Mika hadn't asked why, they were holding their cards close. She didn't blame them and she couldn't complain that she was being used, she'd asked to be part of this

While riding, she'd hoped she'd find Aurin despite knowing his already divided loyalties. She'd wondered if he could be persuaded to help Ackbarr if the Cassin would benefit. Rufus had nodded when she'd mentioned it although she knew he wouldn't make up his own mind until he'd met him. She hadn't been looking forwards to travelling through the mountains on her own either, they were full of dangerous creatures and she couldn't change her skin. Once past Tatton she'd be unable to take any soldiers, the Cassin wouldn't appreciate 'Grengag' knowing where they were and Stafa had been left in Ackbarr due to not being able to keep up with the horses.

There had been many questions about the transcript she'd given them, Varian hadn't spared her feelings and everything had been committed to paper. She'd felt naked afterwards, all her nerve endings raw. It had brought up buried memories, including the difficult conversation she'd had with Lissina's father after she'd come back from the Temple Library. Mika had been summoned by him and still aching with wanting to hold her babies, she'd gone.

She remembered how Lord Dellon had been pacing the small room, she'd only known him from a distance as the man who had allowed his rooms to be used as a tutor for some of the future nobility of Ackbarr. "You killed him."

"Yes." There was no need to ask who he was talking about.

He nodded. "I could not have called him out. He would have killed me for the pleasure of it and I still had my wife to think of." Lord Dellon's face had been stony, new lines around his mouth. "And my daughter, even if she was living elsewhere." She'd felt out of her depth in the older man confiding in her. There were strict codes binding the dukes together, one did not speak like this to a much younger man.

"Lissina was special." It was the only thing Mika could offer him. Lissina had been bright and vivacious, the tutor group hadn't been the same after Mika had come back. Jenna had left to be taught elsewhere and the other boys were in awe of her killing Jace. Studying alone for her journeyman qualifications, she'd felt more isolated than ever.

His hands were clenched, "Girls are different to raise than boys. As a man you want to protect them, prevent the world from ever hurting them." His eyes pierced her, "It is something you will understand if you become a father."

Mika squeezed her own eyes shut, was this part of the reason why she'd tried to protect Lissina for so long? This conversation she'd had with Lord Dellon?

He'd continued, "We both know that my daughter had feelings for you, even if you did not return them. You were good to her." Mika shook her head, opening her mouth to say it was all her fault. He held up a hand, "I understand you have no family here. My wife and I would like to help sponsor you through your journeymanship. I will hear no arguments, I have already spoken to Belindros about it and he agrees."

There was nothing she could do, only bow her head and thank him. That money had helped, enabling her to pay Lin a rent to live at his house even if he refused it. There'd been no option of living with Varian as she was supposed to, both of them had acknowledged that they liked their privacy too much.

What would have happened if Jace had stayed in the mountains? So many events had been linked into a chain of misfortune. It couldn't have been just Jehanne changing that had pushed him, he could have stayed away from her. Like it or not, her own life and his was bound between all three peoples, Cassai, Cassin and Ackbarr.

She stayed in her room for the rest of the evening, ignoring calls for meals and stared out of the window, wishing there didn't have to be war.

Chapter 5

Mika walked into the sick room the next morning to find Tamar sitting on the edge of Aurin's bed. Aurin had been propped up and was sipping soup from the spoon Tamar was patiently holding against his lips.

He tried to smile and failed, "No more… Please." It was a whisper, barely heard. Aurin turned his face away from the spoon and Tamar stopped. Aurin's eyes were bloodshot, the blue looking strange under the darker hair and bruises.

"I'll leave you two." Tamar put the bowl on the table and closed the door quietly. He'd learnt discretion over the last few years, even if his chatter hadn't appeared to have lessened.

Mika came to sit in Tamar's place. "How do you feel?"

His arm had been unshackled, Mika guessed he was in no fit state to run even if he wanted to. "I've been better." He shifted and Mika propped up his pillows further behind him. "All that training just to fluff pillows."

It was a weak joke. "I'll get you back for that one when you're able to stand up on your own. What happened?"

"I was rushing, made a few too many mistakes and got caught by the workers. Maksim's sergeant came just in time, his soldiers were going to hang me." His face twisted. "Thankfully he decided it was best for his overlord to decide what to do with me." She didn't believe him, there had to be more. He could've allowed his horse to trample his attackers, fought them off with the sword he wore.

"There was still a mob at the gates when I came. I don't blame them, people have died because of Cassai Aurin."

"Yes, it was Dulcin's plan. It didn't quite go as he wanted it to. I think he wanted the city to fall and then Cassai could throw off Ackbarr's yoke. Maybe he felt that other states would do the same and Ackbarr would lose all its power."

"He should have got rid of the Medici as well then and many of the states know they're better off under Ackbarr."

"He doesn't think like that. He's getting old Mika, and desperate." He yawned, shifting and winced.

"You need to rest again."

"He knows about the road Mika." He reached for her as she helped to lift him down on the bed. "He knows that Ackbarr wants to invade, that's why I was sent."

"To spy?"

"He wanted me to infiltrate the palace…" His eyes were closing despite his fighting the sleep. "To kill who I could.." Aurin's face slackened and reluctantly Mika raised his good arm and shackled him back to the bed. She couldn't take any risks at the moment.

Mika wandered downstairs, wondering if she could stomach breakfast when Maksim stopped her.

"My lady would like to see you in her sitting room."

Despite her misgivings over Aurin, she smiled and said, "I'd be delighted, I hear congratulations are in order." An uncharacteristic grin split the sombre Medici's face as she clapped him on the shoulder. "I'll go and see her."

The upper rooms in the keep had changed further since Mika had last stayed there. Lissina's touch was everywhere, the hangings and little sophistications unique to Ackbarr city that she'd brought from her parents. It might have been a rich lord's hunting residence rather than a year round home. The servants were local and spoke with a country burr but Mika could tell Lissina had been training them well. She blinked when Lissina appeared in a set of soft red dresses rather than her usual grey. The colour suited her and she said so.

Lissina flushed, "Maksim likes me in this colour and I felt it was time for a change." She touched her stomach, "I was going to write, did Tamar tell you?"

"You know Tamar, talks about everything but the important stuff but he did say eventually."

She laughed, "Well, you're here now and you know."

Mika felt a delight rising at the thought of being able to sink into a purely feminine conversation. She sat in the other chair by the fire and leant forwards, "You're lucky, you've got two Medici here to cosset you."

"They have been. Maksim's not allowed me to lift a finger since I told him and Tamar's nearly as bad." Lissina looked shy, "Actually Mika, would you help me when it's my time? Tamar's like a little brother to me and well, Maksim…" She trailed off.

"I'd love to Lissina, but did you know that Rufus is planning to go to war?"

Lissina bit her lip, "Are you going as well?"

"I have to…" Her heart nearly broke at the way Lissina took a breath and held it. They were both tangled in the same web, Mika had thought by marrying Maksim she'd stepped out of it but the echoes were still there.

"If you can come, will you?"

"Of course." She tried to lighten the conversation, "I could bring Rosita down, did you know the Medici are starting to take on girls as a matter of course now?"

"Due to Rosita?"

"Well," Mika had to be honest. "It helps that she's bright and has shown that girls can deal with anything the boys can but it's also due to there not being a huge number of available boys around."

Lissina beamed, "See, I told you…" At Mika's look she laughed, "And how is Rosita?"

"We had a little trouble with her education at the slaughter house but any objections were stopped once I went in with her."

"Does she know about you being a woman as well yet?"

"No." Mika sobered, "She's still so young…"

"Tamar knew, and Jon. They were young too."

"That's different, they had to know. I don't like letting these things out unless I have to."

"Promise me that you'll tell her one day, it'll mean a lot to her."

Mika shrugged a shoulder, "One day." One day she'd not be able to hide her sex, the cat would take over and not care. She tried to change the subject, "So when is the baby due and what are you hoping for?"

"Autumn, and Maksim's told me he wants a little girl to cuddle." They shared a laugh as a servant knocked to come in with a small tray of food. Lissina thanked him and said, "Maksim already spoils me at every opportunity, I'm going to get fat."

"And he'll love you even more for it." There'd been a time when Mika would have been jealous of her friend – not now. "So, tell me everything." She grabbed a pasty and settled herself down for an enjoyable morning, free from any worries about war or ex-lovers.

Aurin stood before Rufus, his good wrist had been strapped to the wide leather belt around his waist, the broken arm was fastened to a loop first running around his neck and then behind him to the same belt. It was three weeks since Mika had first seen him and his bruises had faded. The dressings had been taken off and with the angry red scar marking his face and broken nose, he wouldn't be so un-noticeable now. His days as a spy were numbered.

The journey hadn't been easy, getting the wagon through the peasants had taken all the guards working together and rumours of the Cassai spy had spread fast. They'd travelled as quickly as they could, sleeping rough and lightly. It had been hard on Aurin, he'd gritted his teeth and endured the jouncing about.

He'd been given a room in one of the towers, not quite a cell but near enough. There was no furniture apart from the bed and no way out apart from the door guarded by trusted soldiers. He'd tolerated the conditions, aware he had little choice.

Rufus had watched him come into the room, taking in the injuries and the limp. "Mika has spoken to me about you. Why should I trust you?"

"My grandmother was Cassin, unlike Mika she couldn't change and although she escaped to the mountains with them, she couldn't stay once they realised her disability." Rufus snorted and Aurin continued, a defiant spark in his eye. "She was escorted to a safe place in Cassai and left there to make her own living. Her daughter went with her and ended up on the docks, drinking away her sorrows and joined by my father when he wasn't on his ship. My father was an Ackbarr sailor, I get my hair from him."

Rufus squinted at Aurin's dyed hair, "You're half Cassai?"

"Cassin," Aurin had his chin up, "My mother was also Cassin not Cassai and I have red hair under the dye, Mika can vouch for that." Mika felt herself flush under Rufus' speculative glance. "My mother spent her life either drunk or scared and as a consequence I grew up fast. When she was finally found by the Cassai elite, she slit her throat." Aurin clenched his fists, "She'd heard too many stories about what would happen to her and she kept her hair bleached as closely as she could to blend in. Those in charge like to keep tabs on any who have the bloodlines, I was taken in and 'educated' in a similar way to Mika's brother, Petron. Unlike him, I simply mouthed my obedience and made myself useful. When I was let off the leash, I found my way to the mountain kingdom and the Cassin. Jehanne's mother was still alive at that point and I proved myself to them. I've been helping them in any way I can since that point."

"Why?"

"My mother and grandmother had fond memories of their time there. The Cassin are very family orientated, they never found anything like that elsewhere." There were lines of bitterness around Aurin's mouth.

Mika volunteered, "Despite the fact that Aurin was employed by Dulcin, he was trusted enough to look for Selene when she went missing, she's Jehanne's daughter."

"That's the girl Tamar liked?" He'd insisted Tamar come back with them, much to Tamar's disgust. Rufus had spent several evenings closeted with his little brother, interrogating him. Tamar had come out to drink with Jon and Mika afterwards, refusing to say much.

"Yes."

Rufus made his decision in his typical swift way, "I'll trust you up to a point. You'll stay in your rooms for the moment until I've decided what to do. If I find you out of them without an escort, I'll throw you to the city's mercies. It won't be pretty."

Aurin nodded slowly and said dryly, "Thanks, I've had that experience already, I'm not eager to repeat it. Mika told me that you want to speak to Jehanne?"

"Tell her I want to speak to her in person, I have a proposal for her and tell her to bring her daughter as well."

Mika got off her horse with a sigh, she'd had a summons from Rufus several days ago to pack and ride with him. She'd had an uncomfortable couple of hours discussing her involvement with a panel of Medici, although Medici were responsible for themselves, anything that took them away from their duties had to be talked through.

She'd also briefly re-talked through her time in the Cassin stronghold to Rufus with Aurin filling in the large gaps in her knowledge. She could tell he was holding nothing back, his desire to have his revenge driving him. Rufus had been impressed by the idea of the fortress in the mountains, although he was less enamoured by the idea of the Weaven trees. He'd seen the one Jon had brought back and the complicated system they had for feeding and keeping it in one place – it wasn't an easy job.

Aurin had been sent off with a contingent of guards several weeks ago. He'd not been allowed to re-dye his hair or skin on the way back and the guards had been as much to protect him as make sure he went off in the right direction. A message had been relayed back to Rufus that Jehanne would be waiting in the keep at Tatton.

Mika kept meat back from the meal for Stafa, she'd insisted he follow her this time despite knowing he'd be tired and irritable from travelling so fast. There was no option for him to ride in one of the supply carts but she wanted him close in case Hal was around. It was strange, she'd not felt bothered by any of the other Cassin males but Hal was different and she didn't know how far gone he'd be.

Stafa appeared late in the evening and flopped down at her side, snarling at any who came near. Rufus spent the evenings staring into the flames, nearly as irritable as Stafa. Mika could tell he was mulling ideas over in his head, working out complicated moves in a dangerous game. One wrong step could cost thousands more lives, including his own and those of his wife and children. Only success would placate the dukes, failure would be fatal.

She stole a look at Tamar, he'd been looking relaxed throughout the ride, apparently uncaring that his older brother had sacrificed him for an alliance with the Cassin. He'd always known he would be married for political gain and was happy so long as he could practice his chosen profession.

The Medici on the other hand, had objected to Rufus using one of their own for political reasons until Tamar had mildly pointed out that he didn't mind seeing as it was Selene he was marrying. The fact that he was also close to qualifying and it got the Medici a foothold in a new country were minor points. Mika noticed his certificate had come very quickly after that and he now wore his new robes with delight.

Mika rubbed her left hand, remembering the cut that had been made when she'd married Rylan. It could barely be seen and yet she could still feel the shock she'd had when the knife had sliced and her palm pressed against that of her new husband. The twist of the ropes binding them and the events leading up to his death. Rufus had agreed to a similar ritual. The Cassin didn't care much for formal ceremonies, who cared when you could threaten to rip out the throat of any who upset you?

Few others knew of the marriage yet – another reason for the hurry. Mika knew there would be shrieks of upset from some of the noble ladies at the thought of the last of Rufus' brothers marrying. Tamar caught her glance and smiled. Stafa briefly opened his eye to rumble an exhausted warning at him coming to sit next to her and went back to sleep, his heavy head resting on her outstretched legs. She ran her fingers lightly over his neck, feeling him relax and winced at the weight.

"You've been watching me a lot, you're wondering how I'm coping?" He spoke quietly.

"You're not talking, it's always a bad sign."

Tamar ducked his head as he chuckled in agreement. "I don't think either of us have much choice."

"Selene's a pain in the behind, she's not going to fit in with Ackbarr society and she'll take it out on you."

"And this is from her half-sibling." Tamar deliberately didn't mention sister. He sobered, "I know, she'll have to come back to Ackbarr to begin with. After everything's sorted, we'll find somewhere else. I had been Maksim's heir and it would have made sense to live there, but I don't think that'll happen now." He spoke as if the war was a minor inconvenience.

"You mean Lissina and Maksim's child?"

"Of course. It'll be lovely to see their baby."

“Looking forwards to being an honorary uncle?” He grinned, a flash of teeth in the firelight. “You could be having your own children with Selene.”

“Cassin women don’t become pregnant easily, I don’t expect anything Mikon.” He looked a little sad at the thought. Mika knew that one well enough, after all this time she’d only carried the twins to term. The Cassin were terribly inbred and their own problems of changing didn’t help. She wondered if knowing that would have helped her in Fenin before she’d changed for the first time. She shook her head, nothing would have changed Rylan’s behaviour and her response had been due to grief and shock. Tamar looked querying at her head shake and she smiled back at him.

“Let’s hope, hey?”

They clattered through the small town with ragged children pointing and running alongside the soldiers. Rufus scattered coins with an absently generous hand and Mika recalled her own introduction into giving alms for those poorer than herself. The workers were back in the fields, Mika had seen them glancing up as they’d ridden by. Lord Maksim had closed his lands at Rufus’ request and taken the offer of compensation to do so.

Maksim must have been keeping a look out for them, he came to greet them as they dismounted and his steward immediately began to show the men where to take their horses. Someone took Mika’s horse and she greeted Maksim with warmth, wondering how Lissina was coping with their visitors. He gave a short bow to Rufus and invited him in. Mika followed them closely.

Rufus walked in as though he owned the place and stopped at the various dark blond heads lounging at the table. Mika was relieved not to see Hal amongst them. She could see Rufus measuring the Cassin up and saw the way they twisted to look at him, noting his own stance. In comparison to the servants around them, they didn't look quite human and she wondered if people saw her in the same way.

Jehanne stood and strode over, she'd not changed much in the last three years. Still in tunic and trousers and with her hair cut short, she held out her hand to Rufus, an amused look in her eye. "You must be Rufus." No titles were given or asked for.

"A good guess." He pulled out his own considerable charm, giving her a rakish smile and shook her hand.

She laughed, "Not really, I've had practise at spotting alphas. I'm Jehanne." She held her arms out to Mika and hugged her hard. Close up, Mika could see the crow's feet around her eyes and a tiredness in her face that hadn't been there before. She felt a panic, Jehanne didn't have long and by association, neither did she. "It's good to see you again."

"How are Rey and Deon?"

"You can ask them yourself. They came with us."

"And Kaylan?"

Jehanne's face closed, "He has settled into one body completely."

Mika felt a grief rising, her brother was no longer human. The easy arrogant teenager of their shared past was no more, even having him as a nearly mute adult had been something. The man who'd sat beside her, communing with the night, her twin, had left her behind and she would follow him shortly into bestiality. She swallowed it down, now was not the time to grieve.

Jehanne gave her an understanding squeeze and turned to wave her hand, "Selene should be here in a minute."

"I'm here now."

Selene stood close to the stairs, her stance belligerent. She was in a tunic and trousers, her feet bare and her sandy blonde hair flowing over her shoulders. Mika could see the men coming into the hall eyeing her up and remembered the problems Dabora had caused simply by wearing split trousers and a sword. Ackbarr's elders were going to go into fits when Selene arrived.

"That's her?" Rufus muttered. At Mika's murmured assent, he chuckled, "The squirt's going to have his hands full."

"And he'll enjoy it too." Mika raised her voice, "Hello Selene." She expected Selene to come in with her usual swagger and was surprised when she didn't. It was only when Mika saw the movement that she realised why. She had a small child clinging to her leg and staring up at the armed men. Selene caught her stare and raised her chin. The child was slender and tall for her age, the height was obviously Cassai and yet she had the dark hair and complexion of Ackbarr. The combination was breath taking in a child of two.

"Hang on, is that brat hers? Jehanne, we'll need someone else, we can't have any…" Rufus had spotted the child and not knowing about that part of his little brother's history was coming to his own conclusions.

"Shut up," Mika muttered. He drew his brows down as she glared at him. "Where's Tamar?"

"Here." Tamar blinked, adjusting his eyes to the darker hall. "Have you seen…" He stopped as he saw Selene and spotted the child. "Oh." He limped further into the room, his eyes only for the young woman by the staircase.

Rufus muttered, “He’s lost.” He still didn’t know what was happening, he could just see the two in front of him ignoring everyone else.

Tamar asked, “Why didn’t you say?”

“Nothing to do with you until now. She’s called Tahiri.” Selene’s face was diffident as she picked her daughter up to show Tamar. Mika saw the contrast in the way her hands held the small girl – she cared a lot. The Cassin were very family orientated, it was built into them with the changing. She remembered her own struggle in letting go of her babies, she could only have done it because her parents had offered to look after them.

Tamar reached a hand out, smiling. “Hello Tahiri.” The child twisted and put her face into Selene’s shoulder. He brushed her back as though not believing it. He swung around to face the rest of the room, “This is my daughter Tahiri. I’m claiming her now, before the wedding in case anyone doubts she’s mine.” He had a fierce determination in his face.

“She’s not yours to claim, she’s mine,” Selene glared at Tamar.

Aurin stepped in, “It’s different here Selene, Tamar claiming her means she’s not illegitimate.” The soft bronze of his hair shone in the light, contrasting with the darker blonds.

“What the fuck?” While the others were arguing, Rufus had turned to Mika for an explanation, it was obvious that Tamar hadn’t told him and it hadn’t been something Varian had been told about to write about in his appraisal.

Mika gripped his arm, “Remember I told you Tamar had a broken heart when we came back from Tatton? It was Selene, this is why he didn’t object to the marriage. This child is his, I can vouch for that. The women have the right to choose and Selene wouldn't have gone anywhere near another man from here." She lowered her voice, "And certainly not after Tamar."

Selene was still spitting. Jehanne and the other Cassin were watching with bemusement, illegitimacy wasn't something they worried about in the matriarchal society. Mika could see Rufus working things out and knew they were fortunate that he didn't have the strict mindset most had.

He nodded sharply, "Acknowledged. Congratulations little brother." Tamar relaxed and Maksim stepped in to start showing people their rooms.

Chapter 6

Tamar was down in the hall early the next morning when Mika got up. He was sat at the long table with his new daughter in his lap, having spent a long time getting to know her the previous day. Tahiri was giggling at the noises Tamar was making to get her to eat her breakfast.

Mika sat next to them and picked at a slice of bread. She teased him, "I remember when you were shocked by the number of illegitimate children your brother had."

Tamar refused to have any of it, "She's not illegitimate, she's mine and I won't have her tarred with the same brush. Besides, Rufus has acknowledged most of his bastards."

Mika tried pushing him for more information, "How are you going to cope in Ackbarr? Selene hasn't lived in a city before." She couldn't see Selene coping with the restrictions in dress or manners.

"We'll only live there until the invasion's over. Selene and Tahiri need to be safe. Having thought about it, I'm intending us to live in Cassai afterwards. I'll give up my claim to my lands and Rufus will compensate me. This place will go to Maksim and Lissina's child. I want to learn from both the Cassai and Cassin, they all have so much information we don't know about. I'll work with anyone willing."

He'd be a foreigner in a hostile land, he was related to the War Duke who was due to invade their country and married to a Cassin - someone acknowledged as an animal by the ruling elite in Cassai. "You're going to have a lot to contend with Tamar."

His dark eyes flashed, “I know, I can deal with it.” He was quietly stubborn under his easy going exterior. “I faced down my father to follow my own path, I can do this too.” Tamar’s arms tightened around his daughter and Mika saw a fierce protectiveness showing for the first time. He’d suffered bullying as a child for his club foot in a warrior society that prized aggression from its men and had fought his own battles to study as a Medici. He loosened his arms and smiled down at his daughter, tickling her to make her laugh. “Isn’t she gorgeous? She looks like Selene.” Tahiri’s face was elfin under the shock of dark hair and her level brows suggested she might have inherited stubbornness from both her parents. Tamar was going to have his hands full keeping them both balanced.

“She’s beautiful, and she looks like you too.”

“Really?” His own smile was brilliant.

Mika clapped him on the shoulder, “Yes, she does Tamar.” She stood, leaving the shredded bread on her plate. “I’m going to look for my own offspring, see you later.”

She nearly walked into Lissina as she came out into the courtyard. A few others were outside, doing the daily chores of the keep and the smells of human habitation clung in the morning air. Lissina looked tired and she sent her maid inside at the sight of Mika.

“How are you coping with the Cassin?”

“Actually, better than I thought. Maksim told Jehanne that I’d had problems and why and she’s kept the men away. They don’t tend to like being in here anyway. It’s warm weather and they’ve been sleeping outside. They are younger too, they don’t remind me so much…” She trailed off. Cassin men all looked very alike, tall, slim and sandy haired.

"And you're coming out when they aren't."

"Yes. I don't want to feel trapped in my own home but I don't want to see them either."

"Just a few days and then you can have your home back." She squeezed Lissina's hands and left her to her walk.

Outside the gates the early morning was stunning, the air was clear and it went to her head. She could feel the cat twitching, wanting to explore the familiar trails to find out if anything had changed. She soothed it with a promise for later. It rebelled - it wanted out now. There was no chance to persuade it otherwise, Mika sobbed and ran for the trees, diving into the cover to lie in the leaf litter.

The shiver as her skin partially grew fur and her face pushed out into a muzzle. The cat sniffed the leaves, pushing at them with her nose. A twitch in the corner of her mind and she rolled over to see Stafa pacing out of the keep. He'd arrived early last evening, snarled at the Cassin in the hall and sprawled against her, marking her as his own. She'd had a relief seeing him despite her usual irritation at his possessiveness.

Stafa walked down the track, the wind was in her favour and the cat brought her hind legs silently underneath her, unconsciously trying to twitch the tail that wasn't there. He flicked his own tail, he knew she was somewhere close. Despite herself, Mika couldn't help joining in with the cat's mischief. She noticed the slide of muscle under his skin, his ears rotating to catch every sound. She was on his blind side, she bared her teeth and sprung for him, twisting as he leapt to one side. Something caught her as she landed, it was too fast for Mika's human brain to catch but the cat swiped and caught another cat.

She was buried under an avalanche of fur, sheathed claws and mock biting. Two cats, both older juveniles, she shook them off as the cat retreated in a huff. Mika changed back and sat panting, beginning to laugh at the two facing her. They were both unusually dark furred in contrast to Stafa's grey and with gleaming blue green and hazel eyes.

Mika looked at Stafa, "I take it you knew?" He licked his nose and looked away and she rolled her eyes, so much for her surprise. "Hello you two, are you going to change so we can talk?"

Her sons disappeared and came back, both were dressed in a pair of trousers in a worse state for being carried. Mika stood and discovered they were taller than her and hugged them in delight. They reciprocated with a shyness, she was an aunt to them and one they'd only met once. A twitch in her mind and another grey furred cat slid out of the bushes.

"Kaylan." He blinked at her and put the rabbit down that he was carrying. Stafa went across and they nuzzled each other briefly in welcome. Kaylan began gutting the rabbit and it disappeared in short order. Mika tried to ignore the crunching of bones as her own cat reminded her of the chase and spurt of hot blood.

"Papa doesn't change anymore." There was sadness in Rey's voice.

"Jehanne told me. Can you still understand him?"

Deon shrugged, "He's still there but not so interested. We're important but not." He scrubbed a hand over his eyes and looked away.

Kaylan was licking the blood away from his paws. Apart from the fact he was sat so calmly in their presence there was nothing to say he wasn't an ordinary forest cat,. Stafa sniffed and then began to clean the other cat's muzzle. Kaylan raised his head, his eyes half closed, enjoying the grooming.

"Jehanne says it's going to happen to us too."

"It's the price we pay for being able to change Rey. Would you give that up?" She saw his fists clench, it hadn't been so long ago since he'd been stuck watching his twin change and been unable to follow. "It's what we get for living two lives. We all face the same."

"Aren't you worried? The Cassin don't."

She couldn't answer that one, it stung too much. "They've lived with the knowledge all their lives, we haven't and your Papa never knew any different."

"Papa changed early, will we…?"

Mika shook her head, "No, your Papa was kept in his cat shape for too long by an alpha, he lost himself." She told them the story from the knowledge she'd had at the time, not telling them that she was their mother. She'd made up a story that a woman had come to Belindros after Kaylan's death, mistaking Mika for her twin brother. She daren't tell them that she was their mother, they'd lose her shortly too.

They were quiet afterwards. Mika surreptitiously gazed at her sons, seeing flashes of her lover and their father Ezra in their faces and movements. A pang, those stolen nights felt an age away. They were very similar to Tahiri in their colouring, both of them had dark hair and the Ackbarr olive skin. She wondered how much of herself was in them - that was harder for her to see apart from the obvious height and slimness.

The cats had sprawled out and were dozing in the spring sunshine. Deon brightened, "Well, at least we're going back into Cassai. We might find Mamet and Koren." Koren had been quite open about not being their grandfather to the twins, with both Kaylan changed and Mika supposedly dead there hadn't been a need.

"You're not going to be part of whatever Rufus has planned are you?" For the first time she had a mother's worries about her sons. They were sixteen and thought they were invincible, war was nothing to them. It wasn't just the idea of them getting hurt, she didn't want them with blood on their hands.

"We all are, there aren't enough of us not to." Deon looked uncomfortable at her concern. Despite their delight at seeing her, she was only an aunt they'd met for a few months.

Rey added, "We'll stay out of trouble and we have Papa. He stays around even if he can't talk or change anymore."

Mika left them, worrying about their part to come in this war Rufus was planning and wondered if Jehanne could keep them away from any action and swore to herself. The boys were right, there were far too few of them. She closed her eyes, a lot of people were going to get killed. She'd never thought about Rufus' abilities on the battlefield, despite hearing about his campaigns in the uneasy lands over the northern water. All the stories that had been relayed in the taverns and whispered in the keep about his skirmishes and out thinking his opponents. How did the Medici sent out to help deal with all this deliberate hacking apart of people? She drew a sharp breath, and the next lot of people would be hers to deal with.

Stafa leant against her leg and chirruped. Her fingers found the deep ruff. It felt wrong, but she knew Cassai had stepped over the line in human politics. The threatened invasion of her country was finally going to happen. Could she have ever foreseen herself on the invaders side all those years ago? Mika opened her mouth and panted in distress, not caring that the cat was coming through – no one was here to see. Jon was back in Ackbarr and no one waited for her at the keep.

She ran hands through her hair that curled into claws, pads thickening her slender fingers. Never a complete change, a mockery of what she should be. Her vision dimmed into monochrome, her hearing sharpening. Stafa leapt forwards in a bound that teased her into chasing him, showing his flank in a ripple of smooth muscle. The cat pushed through her awareness and sprang after him as Mika sank into oblivion.

She lay, panting in the sun, a lethargy with the warmth creeping through her bones. The cat released her, sated and Mika sat up to look around, she was on the rocks overlooking the deep valleys before the plains. Stafa rolled over, exposing his paler belly, his legs akimbo. She'd lost most of the day by the looks of it. She couldn't blame the cat for taking advantage, she had no timetable of duties here, no restrictions on when she had to be in certain places. There was a regret in her mind for all the earlier times when she'd fought the cat for control. She felt rested, the looming conflict had been pushed away as insignificant.

A noise in the trees to one side and she jerked her head up, the cat's senses still underlying her thought processes. Stafa barely twitched. A tall figure pushed through and pulled his hood down, smiling.

"I heard you went out early." Aurin hadn't re-dyed his skin or hair and the soft bronze caught the light. "Enjoy your hunting?"

"Fat lot of good you are." Mika nudged the large cat with her foot and he groaned, his good eye firmly shut. She raised her voice, "How did you guess?" She had a horror of not changing back properly and tried to stop herself from glancing down.

"You've got blood on your shirt." He chuckled as she noticed the splatters across her clothes in dismay and sat next to her on the rock, raising his own face to the sun. The red seam of his scar still made her wince.

"Haven't you a guard to keep you out of mischief?" The comment was barbed, he wasn't supposed to be wandering around unattended, none of the Cassin were although in practice it wasn't working. They simply slipped out with a look at the keep guards.

"Jehanne has spoken to Rufus and he agreed that I don't need one. I'm not going anywhere Mika, Dulcin is going to pay for what he's done." Aurin's voice was determined. He'd been quiet the previous evening, she noticed his hands clenching around his cup at times while he watched from his corner. "Anyway, I came to find you to say keep Stafa beside you when you get back to the keep."

"Why?"

"Hal will be arriving in the next day or so. Don't trust him, he's degenerated further in the last few years. Jehanne can control him but even she struggles at times."

"Shit." She remembered the large muscular man walking through the corridors of Dobrin and how he'd noticed her. She shivered, the comparison between him and her biological father pulling her into changing wasn't to be considered. "Do you think he'll be a problem?"

He tilted his head, “For you with Stafa around probably not. Just let Rufus know to back off around Jehanne.”

“What do you mean?”

He sniggered, “Haven’t you noticed? They’ve been at it like rabbits.” Mika wasn’t quite sure what to think. She was aware that Rufus had discrete dalliances on the side and that Keira also probably knew but still… Aurin sobered, “I’m not sure it’s good for Jehanne, although she’s probably enjoying it at the moment. Hal’s not changed for a good eighteen months and Jehanne’s resisted following him. She really wants the Cassin to get back into Cassai Mika. I hope Rufus’ not making promises he’s not going to keep.”

“Rufus generally keeps his promises.” She was still a little stunned by the news of Rufus and Jehanne.

Aurin touched her face, bringing her attention back to him, “I can understand his fascination, Cassin women have something about them.”

Mika flushed, despite his broken nose and the still red scar down his face, he’d not lost the ability to make her stomach twist. “I’m still with Jon. I’m not like Rufus, Aurin.”

“Shame. Just a kiss for old time’s sake?” His lips were as warm as she remembered them and she held herself back with an iron grip. A low growl startled them both and Aurin jerked back as he noticed Stafa’s lambent eye on him. Stafa and Jon had a truce these days, Aurin was obviously not included in it. “What’s with him? I’ve heard he’s not a changer.” He smiled nervously.

“Give me a few years and it won’t matter.” Mika tried to keep her voice level and failed. “He’s stubborn. He knows he only has to wait.”

Aurin opened his mouth to say something and then shut it again. He tried, “At least with the invasion you may be able to settle back in Cassai.”

The forests called - sliding through green shadows, gnats buzzing across limpid pools. She unconsciously stretched her muscles, taking every movement in. The power to rend and tear compressed into an ability to make the slightest delicate twitch of her whiskers. The cat stretched out a paw, for once asking nicely.

“Mika?”

Mika jumped, “Sorry.” The cat slid away, affronted at the interruption.

He regarded her with concern, “Jehanne slides off like that.”

She didn’t need to know that, and it had been happening more often recently. Mika glanced upwards, checking the sun. Food would ground her. “I’m hungry.” She saw Aurin’s look and qualified, “For food, nothing else.” Mika forced down the knowledge that a male body making her pay attention to herself would do a similar thing. Maybe that was why Jehanne was open to Rufus’ advances.

Not wanting to think further, Mika snapped her fingers. “Coming Stafa?” The large cat rolled over with another groan and shook himself. He blinked his resentment and followed her to the keep.

Mika looked around carefully for Hal when she arrived and didn’t see him. The servants were walking around the Cassin as though they might bite. The few Cassin there lounged at the tables, mostly ignoring them. Mika eyed them up, they were all youngsters, a few years older than her sons. Old enough to be steady and reasonably trustworthy but not old enough for their inner cats to have taken over.

She sat at a table on her own, feeling out of place with what should be her own countrymen. She wondered at her ability to feel content with those in Ackbarr, Jehanne had mentioned that few were interested in learning or their history. Was she a further freak in her pursuit of learning? Her brother had never been interested either, preferring physical and outdoor pursuits even as a child.

So many hours spent sitting at her table, she could almost feel one of the books in front of her. The touch of her fingers across the pages, the sounds of the city outside and the light in the room, she'd been reading it before she'd left. Which book was it… her mind reached out for the answer and drew a blank.

Mika thumped her hand down on the table, ignoring the looks given by others in the room. She could bluff her way through lessons, kidding her students so they guessed what she was going to say. It was a game she'd become known for but she couldn't lie to herself – she was losing her memory and she hated it. Every little gap was another step into her degeneration. She knew she would remember later on and it would feel like another smack in the face.

She got up to collect a bowl and scooped some stew into it. A servant offered wine and she shook her head, she needed her wits about her. In a foul mood, she watched as Rufus walked in with Jehanne. Now that Aurin had mentioned it, Mika could see the connection between them. The slight smile on Jehanne's face and the contented swagger in Rufus' walk. She swore, if others could see then she was going to have to mention it. Jehanne went to sit with her countrymen. Rufus caught Mika's eye and grinned as he grabbed a plate and came to sit next to her. She felt like slapping him.

"What's up?" He looked amused at her mood.

"You need to watch yourself." She knew she sounded snappy and that he'd think it was to do with Jehanne. She explained, "Jehanne's mate Hal is an alpha and he makes Stafa look like a house cat. Apparently he'll be arriving soon."

Rufus shrugged easily, "Will he cause trouble?"

"Aurin mentioned he doesn't like competition, even having the extra soldiers around could set him off. I'm hoping Jehanne will keep him happy." She refused to let anything out other than a veiled warning.

He nodded and she could see he'd taken it on board. "I've spoken to the soldiers, they are aware of the habits of the Cassin and have been told not to react if they see the women walking round naked."

"It's not going to be easy, the Cassin have very different standards."

"Tough, I'm paying them to behave." Mika snorted and he took a sip of his wine, unbothered by his own behaviour. They finished their meal quietly and when Jehanne came over, Rufus stood, lazily smiling. Mika refused to be part of the conspiracy between them and left to find Lissina.

Chapter 7

Mika elbowed the door open and Stafa slid through first, making her swear as her saddlebags slipped off her shoulder.

"I'm back." The call fell flat as she saw Jon sat at the table, his head in his hands. "What's up?" Part of her noticed that Stafa had pushed open the door to her bedroom and had climbed on her bed and she swore at the thought of more cat hair on her bed.

"The old bastard finally died." Jon's voice was flat. "I thought he'd died years ago, I never heard from him. An old acquaintance recognised him and contacted me."

"Who?" Mika dragged a chair close and wrapped an arm around him. She felt him relax a little although he didn't move.

"Hanion." The man he'd thought was his father. To say he'd been brought up by him was an over statement, he'd simply been around while Jon had grown up. Then he'd tried to get Jon to steal from Lin's household once Jon had moved in and had kidnapped him when he'd refused.

"Oh Jon," Mika's voice was full of sympathy.

"I was surprised when I found out it was him, there wasn't much left. He never knew I was there." He had a haunted look, "I gave him mercy." The only thing left to give, the drugs wouldn't have helped him if the illness was that far gone. It would have been a painful death otherwise until his vital organs finally gave up. Mercy indeed. Mika rubbed Jon's shoulders. "I hadn't thought of him for years, I suppose blanked it out after I came to live with you and Lin.

"He was never that bad to Ma, he'd swear at me to leave them alone at times and she'd shoo me away. He could be quite funny when he was drunk, he'd show me things and talk but he frightened me as a small child." Mika continued to rub, knowing he had to talk himself out, mourning a man he'd never loved. "I suppose I never knew when he was going to explode and Ma was always on edge around him. Later on, I'd go out into the markets and talk to the traders there. They'd give me food sometimes, I think they felt sorry for me."

Jon carried on in a monotone voice, picking out memories of a hard childhood. His mother cleaning and taking in washing to keep food on the table for them and the few memories he had as a very young child of the Medici's household. Mika let him talk, gently agreeing with him until he came to a stop.

She left a silence and then asked, "I'll make a drink, fancy some tea?"

He nodded, "I didn't know how happy a household could be until I came to live with you. Ma tried her best but…"

"I had the same with my husband. The first evening I arrived in Ackbarr I heard someone singing downstairs. I know you don't have to be happy to sing but it made me feel good. There wasn't any of that in Fenin." Reminiscing like this with Jon, she could almost taste the days of freedom, running from one lesson to the next with the laughter and teasing from her peers.

As though reading her mind, Jon asked, "When have you been happy Mika?"

Mika had to think about it, her teenage years in Ackbarr had been free but over-shadowed by Jace and the pressures of controlling the cat. Since she'd become an adult and a qualified Medici, she'd discovered a different sort of freedom with the ability to make her own decisions. "Actually, this may sound wrong, but I've been happy over the last few years. I know the sleeping sickness has been awful but I've been able to concentrate purely on healing. There's not been any politics."

"I know what you mean… Lin hated politics too."

"And despite the fact that I wanted to become Court Medici, my changing has taken the pressure off in a way that I couldn't. the decision's been taken out of my hands." She caught the wistful look on his face, "And of course there's been living with you."

Jon chuckled, "Fancy a little more happiness?"

"Only a little?" Mika smiled and leant against him.

He kissed the side of her head and wrapped an arm around her, "Forget the tea, I've other ideas to make us feel better."

"No chance of using my bed, someone else is on it." Stafa had commandeered it, sprawled out in an exhausted sleep. She sighed, a fine layer of grey and tan hairs were already on her clean blankets.

"Better use mine then. I'll lock the doors…" Jon smiled and brushed the hair out of her eyes.

Later, she lay against him, enjoying the feeling of his body pressed around hers. "Well, it looks as though Tamar finally got what he wanted."

Jon muttered, "Hmm?"

"He's been married off to Selene and I'm not sure who to feel sorrier for." He chuckled, pulling her closer and she wriggled around until her back was against him. "He's got a daughter from when they were together in the mountains."

"No kidding." Jon was paying attention now.

"It did take some explaining. Tamar hasn't been able to put Tahiri down, he's totally fallen for her." She could feel him smile as he absently brushed his lips against her shoulder. "Saying that, it's just as well this is happening, there's been a bit of controversy." She paused knowing Jon loved any gossip, "Selene's Jehanne's daughter and was due to take over ruling the Cassin however Tahiri is only a half breed."

"So?"

"If she can't change by the time she becomes a certain age then she would have been turned out of the community."

"Like your boys were?"

"Yes, luckily they can both change now." The look in Rey's eyes as she'd pushed him down the slope. She'd never quite forgiven herself even if he had. "Can you see Selene letting her go willingly?"

Jon snorted, "So Jehanne's trying to save her community and her grandchild at the same time. Has Rufus said anything about his plans yet?"

"Well, he and Jehanne spent a lot of time together and I believe there were points when they were only talking…"

"Fuck, did anyone else notice? That could be embarrassing for Keira."

"Not the soldiers, I think the Cassin know but they tend to see these things differently. Did you know that they had no idea about the sleeping sickness until Aurin had mentioned it?"

"They are isolated up there, they're far too busy surviving to worry about the rest of the world."

"Aurin says Petron had been an excuse to upset Ackbarr. They used him Jon."

"Which means they want war and they have a plan. Not good for us."

"I think Dulcin must be desperate. He's getting old."

"Forget old, he must be nearly dead!"

"We have children young, especially in the royal family. He'd be in his eighties probably. Anyway, I don't think Rufus is going to let him get away with it this time. I've no idea what he's planning. The only thing he mentioned is that he'd infected the army. They're immune to the sickness, not decimated like the rumours said."

Jon rolled over to stare at the ceiling, "Rufus is one wily bastard when he wants to be. I think Dulcin will have met his match even if he can hole himself up in Dubari."

"Keira's father wasn't the strategist Rufus is. You remember in the early days of their marriage? Them both playing at Keira barely being in control of him?"

"I think she enjoyed that nearly as much as he did. Tell me Mika, would you marry again if you could?" The question made her freeze coming as it did out of nowhere. He felt her tense and said, "Never mind, forget I asked."

"No, I didn't…"

"I just wish sometimes we could be openly together, not pretending like we do. Don't you wish that sometimes?"

Mika squeezed her eyes tight, thankful her back was to Jon. She knew the soft look that would be on his face and couldn't deal with it. How could she expose herself like that? Having lived as a man for most of her life, she rarely thought of herself as a woman in the way she knew other women did. She couldn't cope with the restrictions…

She tried to be honest, "Yes, I do but I don't think I can cope with the gossip."

"We're two men living together, how can there be any more gossip?" He sighed and pulled her tight body close. "You can't blame me for wondering sometimes. How was Tamar's wedding?"

It took a while for her to be able to answer. The guilt at not being able to give him what he wanted and the acceptance he had of her, that she wasn't even completely human. "Rufus and Jehanne announced on the third day that they'd made a deal. They held it after then."

"You mean she'd finally exhausted him."

The humour caught Mika in her tearful mood and she managed a smile, "Something like that. Tamar had also been nagging Rufus to do something about it."

The tumbledown keep had been quiet after the wedding, most of the Cassin had left the next day for the mountains. Jehanne had embraced Mika when it was time for them to leave. "Keep them safe for me, when I'm not here."

Mika knew she wasn't talking about just Selene and Tahiri. Neither of them knew how long either of them had before humanity was no longer optional. "I'll do my best." She'd tried to smile, "See, it was the right thing for me not to stay. I couldn't have helped if I hadn't been in Ackbarr."

Jehanne's eyes filled with tears and she'd turned away quickly, looking for Hal. She'd walked away, her fingers deep in his ruff and Mika had tried not to think how many times she echoed the same movement with Stafa. Her goodbyes had been equally emotional with her sons. War was looming, and they would be caught up in it as well.

Rufus had spent another day hammering out negotiations with Maksim over the Cassin using his land. Jehanne would be bringing the most vulnerable members of their community out of the mountains so

Rufus could use the rest in his plans. From the sounds of it they would be a pitiful few, mostly youngsters unable to change and a couple of pregnant women. Any who could change completely would be helping when the invasion happened. Mika's stomach clenched again at the thought of her children being in danger.

Jon broke through her thoughts, "Considering Tamar told Selene that Ackbarr wouldn't let them marry the last time they met I'm surprised."

Mika shrugged, "I think that was to make himself feel better. When he found out that Tahiri would be abandoned if she couldn't change, he was horrified. I think Selene was a bit pleased by his reaction."

"Little viper. He's going to have his hands full."

"I think that's the general view anyone has, who's been around them. They were already arguing before we left. He's not letting her get away with anything."

Jon huffed in amusement, his breath warm and Mika closed her eyes. All she wanted to do was be a Medici, have a lover and see her children on occasions. Why did things have to be so difficult?

Chapter 8

Everywhere there was a deathly quiet apart from the waves lapping against the sides of the three ships and the ropes sounding in a now familiar arrhythmic creak. Mika watched the condensation from the fog settle on Stafa's whiskers, sliding down and dripping in a counterpoint to the ropes. He had his ears back, as he had for most of the voyage. Selene had been right to call him stubborn - he'd refused to leave her, walking along the gangplank and glowering at the sailors staring from the rigging.

The air was grey, merging into the grey moving animal that was the sea. Somewhere out there was Cassai and a small out of the way cove that could only be accessed by shallow boats. The other boats were shadows, a man at the bows running a weighted line down to strike the bottom and softly calling that it was clear. The creak of oars were muffled and tilted to make as few splashes as possible.

Silence was the key here, somewhere was the dark green of forest, the birds and animals hunkered down to stay out of this clinging damp. She shifted, pulling her cloak further around herself, her stomach tight and imagined hunters in the undergrowth waiting for them. Ten others, including Jon stood waiting with her and another ten on each of the other two boats. A tiny force and yet they couldn't have more, thirty was already too many in one go. Up and down the coast the same was happening. The fortress in the mountains Rufus had built was a distraction, its soldiers were the old and the lame. The ships pulling the scuttled boats from the Dunbarin harbour at the cost of many sailors would be another diversion, concentrating the Cassai forces in two separate directions.

Rufus had loudly declaimed his anger and threats to sweep through the forests by force, a tactic most unlike him Mika had thought until he'd had finally told those on the ships a good way out to sea, that he planned to take Dubari by stealth, playing Cassai at its own game. The idea was that by the time Cassai realised what was happening, they would have taken Dubari and the royal family. She'd seen Rufus' grin, a flash of teeth in the gloom, he liked pitting himself against an unknown opponent. The not knowing what was happening at the mountain border or Dunbarin was a seasoning to his plans – he wouldn't know if they had worked until they had either succeeded or were captured.

There was no way Mika could have stayed in Ackbarr despite knowing that she would be in the firing line. Jon had come with her, he couldn't let her go without him and they'd needed another Medici to complete their party. He had his own short sword strapped to his side and a buckler. Trained by Gavin, he'd a certain competency unlike Tamar and he'd kept up his training however much he disliked using them.

The quarters had been cramped on the long trip, men tripping over one another and swearing, a forest of swords and other weapons stacked up ready to take with them. The extra pressure of pretending to be a man had been only alleviated by Stafa's presence, the others gave them both space without question. The weather had been usual for this time of year with long balmy evenings and soft winds that turned into misty mornings with the fog dissipating by noon. The fog wouldn't penetrate the forest, but it obscured the sea.

Mika found herself raising her head to snuff the air and stopped with a shake of her head. How many years had it been since she'd been here? It must be over ten. To most here she was a Medici in the prime of her life but to her, the cliff edge of her species showed clearly.

A dark shadow was in front of them and the gentle shush of water on a sandy beach. The man with the leaded rope called out softly and the rowers dipped their oars as he jumped down into the waves to pull the boat up as high as he could. The crunch as it was grounded. Others jumped in to help him and to allow those going into the forest a chance to stay as dry as possible.

Mika jumped, Stafa followed a split second afterwards. He shook a back leg that had slid into the water and twitched his ears, his nose and eyes dilating. With only the slide of the fine gravel betraying him, he disappeared off into the forest. Risone, the sergeant in charge of their little group, looked at Mika in irritation and she shrugged. He'd come back in his own good time.

The other two boats disgorged their men and they were pushed off into the grey dankness. Risone called them up the beach and into the dubious cover of the first trees.

"We wait until the mist has cleared, then we move east." He kept his voice low, "We'll make contact with the Cassin at some point or make our way the best we can. If anyone sees us then we silence them." They all know it would be permanently, no one could afford to get sentimental.

Mika pointed out, "Stafa will probably notice them before we do."

He grunted in response and they settled to wait for the weather to clear, each man checking their bags and equipment. Part of Mika was aware of the forest around her and the familiar noises of her youth. It should have calmed her, it didn't. The sighs and mutters of the men close by, shifting as they tried to find a comfortable position distracted her and she could feel the cat inside, twitching.

Rufus would be further up in a different party, waiting for the mist to lift the same as they were. She checked her rapier, shifting to find a more comfortable spot and sighed. The leather armour creaked, she'd worn it as much as possible after being issued with it but despite oiling it, it still wasn't entirely settled on her. They had all taken the gamble between moving fast and quiet and safety – this armour didn't cover enough to stop a bolt punching through and her countrymen used poison.

Very little noise betrayed their position, she was impressed despite knowing most of these soldiers weren't just trained guardsmen, they were hunters and trackers and the best Rufus could get. They were used to waiting in position for the right moment to send a deadly arrow to their prey. There were others she hadn't been so sure of, more tight-lipped and keeping themselves apart from the rest. They had heavy backpacks that were well padded to stop any betraying clinks and she wondered what Rufus had planned for them.

The rustle of the trees, the smells of the forest, they were reminders of her childhood. Laughing and racing with Kaylan. The shouts as one or the other of them reached some prized position first, grasping the trophy and dancing away with it, catcalling to the other. The walks with Alma, their heads together, the sandy and white blonde hair intermingling. Flashes of her parents - her father dismounting in the courtyard, reaching to swing first one then the other into the air and onto the back of his horse.

And her mother. Mika found tears gathering, remembering her fingers weaving the vineflowers together, the calm she had exuded, the light in her eyes… and now she was gone. As irrevocably dead as Kaylan was. He was aware of her, knew she was important but could never change into human form again.

Mika stood abruptly, aware she couldn't cry in front of the other men. She ignored Risone's sharp look and turned her back on them, staring out into the white. A noise behind her and a touch to her shoulder – Jon giving the only comfort he could.

Her senses expanded as she closed her eyes, the noise of the waves moving across the sand to one side, the mutter of the men shifting and the forest. The damp loam, the subdued calls of birds and the sharp cry of something small and squeaky being pounced on. Mika sighed and opened her eyes, waiting. She shook her head at Jon's questioning look and pointed as Stafa pushed his way through the undergrowth, a limp form hanging from his mouth. He sprawled out and began nuzzling at it. Jon relaxed, chuckling silently. The crunch of bones grounded Mika into reality and she went back to sit with the men, rummaging through her own bag for something to eat.

They spent several days working their way through the forest, everyone on edge and tense. Mika kept herself busy, not allowing the cat a chance to get out and constantly aware of everything around her. They passed several settlements, only small compounds of the kind she recognised, self-sufficient with tiny fields worked by mostly women and teenagers. This was unusual and a testament to the fact that Rufus' plan must be working. The men had to be either at the border or Dunbarin. The women were still in their restrictive clothing although their heads were uncovered. Mika remembered the difficulty in moving and noticed many of the younger girls had their skirts kilted up in the absence of adult men.

Those working in the fields must have been aware of something moving in the forest, no one could live in such close proximity to nature and not notice however the harvest had to be gathered and there was only a short season to do it in. The women ignored the warning cries of birds and carried on, determinedly working. Mika consoled herself by thinking that if Rufus' plan worked, then most of their husbands and fathers would be back to help them soon. The two groups of fifteen foreign soldiers crept past the fields and compounds, unseen under the cover of the undergrowth. No one raised a cry.

The warm humid days under canopy and cool nights made travel difficult. Mika still wore layers to disguise her figure and sweat ran underneath it. There was no privacy to wash herself down, she endured it and stank like the rest of the men. The limpid pools under the shade of trees and rocks bred a million gnats to bite them in the dusk. She showed the men which fruit was edible, pointing out those that weren't with warnings.

The men were chewing on dried meat and bread from their backpacks when Mika heard the warning cries and the silence following. Stafa pricked his ears and went to stand facing a section of forest, his tail twitching. She followed slowly, aware of the men taking notice and putting down their rations. Mika loosened her rapier, she'd not needed it yet. She wondered if she could carry through any actions in cold blood if it proved to be one of her countrymen. Lin had always asserted that soldiers had to frame their mind in a certain way to kill.

She'd killed before, had a man's blood spilling over her hands, warm and wet and with that smell…

Stafa chirruped and turned his back on the forest, his single eye glanced at her once and he went back to his place.

"You're three miles further south than you should be. We've been looking for you all over." The low voice made everyone jump as a tall figure walked out, tying the thong to his kilt. He was as dark blond as Mika and as tall as her brother had been.

"Prove you are what I think you are." Risone walked over to stand next to Mika. He wasn't as tall as the man but was wider in his leather breastplate.

The stranger sneered and held up a hand. It changed, thickening into a cat's paw, the nails curving and darkening. His arm shook and Mika remembered the strain in holding the change. "Happy?"

"What's your name Cassin?"

"Cian." He closed his eyes, ignoring them and Mika heard the call go out. Stafa lifted his head from where he was lying. "You don't need to set sentries tonight, we'll watch you." His arrogance was breath-taking as he settled down against a tree. "I'll take you in the right direction tomorrow."

Risone quirked a look at Mika and she nodded. He gave the hand signal for them to stand down and the men settled although not without some hard looks in the Cassin's direction.

They made fast progress the next day using the forest trails. Mika spotted several shadows flitting past them and pointed them out to Risone. She could hear the calls far and near between the male Cassin, shivering her skin, making her want to change. She ached for the drugs she'd taken in a way she'd not for years, anything to send this part of her to sleep. She found herself eyeing Jon's bag - she knew he had Sweetroot in there.

Despite his arrogance, the Cassin worked with them to tell them when to move and when to stay still. Rufus was taking a risk using them and yet this was an opportunity they would never have had on their own. Jehanne had been open about wanting them to be back where they belonged before they died out completely.

Mika noticed Cian eyeing her as they travelled, he must be aware of her ability to change. He was close to Jon's age, the wildness under his skin calling to part of her that Jon couldn't. It was a similar problem to Aurin, she'd been brought up with men who looked like this, had thought she'd marry one and yet in Ackbarr she was content and happy with Jon. The Cassin side of her wanted to change, to flick her tail at this male and race away, teasing him. Instead she controlled herself with an iron determination.

That evening, knowing that the men were safe, she had a word to Risone and walked away from the group. Standing on her own in the forest, the lush growth surrounding her, she called to her own cat and let it out. Halfway through her change she had to stop, the cat baulking at her constricting corset under the breastplate. She loosened them both and tried again, this time it took over, leaping into the wild.

A noise, she stopped with a hand on the ground and the other raised in anticipation, feeling the muscles almost twitching as the cat tried to move her ears. Stafa burst out and landed on a rock above her. She leapt up, tried to dislodge him and he leapt again. She chased him and they eventually sprawled in a pile at the base of a tree, her fingers running through his fur. He half closed his eye, twisting to lever a heavy paw over her waist. He smelt of forest loam and a rusty rumble started deep from his chest. Mika was allowed to come to the forefront of the mind she shared with the cat and she noticed the difference in herself. She was thicker, her arms more like a cat's although the elbows and knees were still facing the correct way. Maybe she'd be able to change fully soon, part of her hoped that it would be before she lost herself so she could experience being the cat again with a human mind. Shrugging, she slid her body back to her human shape,

Stafa nuzzled at her, a trickle through her mind hinting. Mika slapped at him, relaxed from their playing. "Forget it hairball, I'm still not changed enough." He gave up with good grace and Mika had a brief wonder at what it might be like should she fully change. She could feel her own cat joining in with her curiosity and dragged her mind away from the thought with difficulty.

"If you won't with him, then why not with me?" The voice came from downwind. Both Mika and Stafa lurched up. Cian lounged against a tree, naked in the shadows and giving no doubt to what his interest was in.

Mika swore to herself, she was half dressed and didn't even have a dagger on her. The recollection of Jace trying to force the change made her breath come faster. The knowledge that he'd been half drugged and unable to think clearly didn't help and then she remembered that the Cassin were a matriarchal society – the females didn't tolerate this sort of behaviour.

She deliberately relaxed back against Stafa, "Fuck off Cian, I prefer a man who thinks with his brains not his balls." She rigidly controlled her voice and hated the thought of being reduced to a helpless woman.

“And yet you’re consorting with a beast who cannot change.”

Mika stayed where she was, refusing to move from her embrace. “No shame Cian.” She said calmly, “One day I’ll not change back from the beast either.” Speaking the bald truth soothed her in a way she’d not expected. She couldn’t do anything about eventually changing into a beast but she could choose those she might have around her when she did. Stafa would make a good mate as any at that point.

He narrowed his eyes and Stafa growled, low and threatening. Mika shifted her legs slightly to allow her to be able to throw herself at Cian if she needed to. She tried to figure out how they’d get to Rufus if they had to injure him and what they’d do about the other cats surrounding them without him to control them.

To her surprise, Cian shrugged, “Enjoy your night.” He walked away into the trees, alarm calls sounding above.

Mika stared at the cat lying in her arms, he was longer than she was and heavier. He dropped his head to butt hers, his breath warm against her face. Her anger gave way to upset that she’d been made to feel helpless. She felt the tears rising - and one day she wouldn’t change back. Jehanne had talked of an acceptance, was this the start of it? She had already noticed the holes in her memory, the times she’d laughed it off and asked her students to fill in the gaps as though she’d meant it.

“How long do I have?” Mika said it softly, “How long do you have?” She had no idea how old Stafa was or how many years he had left. The idea that she’d be an animal with no control over who she went with was horrendous. Far better to be with an animal she knew. Mika stroked him fiercely and he lipped at her, enjoying the attention.

“Please wait for me, I need to know you’ll be there.” She wrapped her arms around his neck and cried.

Chapter 9

One hundred and fifty men, most of them Ackbarr, the rest Cassin and all in small groups. There was no time to relax, everything had to go like clockwork - they would be noticed if they stayed for long.

They had joined the main group less than an hour ago, they were the last to arrive. Mika's shoulders had relaxed as she saw the familiar figure of Rufus talking to one of his men. Cian had ignored her and everyone else for rest of the time he'd spent with them, much to Mika's relief. She hated the feeling that she could be made to feel that helpless, that someone knew all her secrets. Jon had stayed close to her, knowing she was upset but unable to talk in the close confines of their group. Stafa had also haunted her footsteps, glaring at Cian whenever he passed too close.

Once reunited with their comrades, the soldiers had split into groups according to their specialities. The men with heavy backpacks had turned out to be engineers and sappers. She heard them talking through their ideas quietly and eyeing up the Cassin who would be leading them. They had maps drawn, but the Cassin could smell their way through the shafts, making escape a lot quicker if needed.

Mika had seen Jehanne, sprawled in an embrace with Hal, not unlike the one she'd been in with Stafa. Jehanne hadn't been talkative and Mika was worried about her. She was going downhill fast, her eyes diffused and her movements echoing those of her mate. The men avoided her and Hal snarled at any who came too close. She wondered if Jehanne was hanging on for some unknown event, maybe the final downfall of the Cassai elite who had enslaved her parents.

No one was in chain mail, the jingle would betray them and plate was too heavy. Everyone wore boiled leather which may or may not be enough to protect from the small repeater bows used by the Cassai. Certainly any exposed part was vulnerable to the toxins used on the tips. Mika shuddered, not even she would be able to save a man hit and without being able to change, she would be as vulnerable as they were.

The group re-split as the Cassin took the engineers and sappers across the hillside to the ventilation shafts. The hunters followed, quietly despatching any Cassai sentries. The Cassai would know something was up by the time they were due back but they wouldn't know what. By that point, they would have their sappers doing their work deep into the bowels of the complex.

Rufus turned to Jehanne, "We're relying on you to keep us safe."

She twisted her head like she was going to lick her shoulder and nodded instead. "We'll do it to get our country back." Rufus looked as if he was going to say something and stopped.

There were few sentries, Mika guessed most of them were either in Dubari waiting for the blocked port to be attacked by Rufus army or at the fortress he'd built in the mountains. She had to hand it to him, Rufus was using Cassai's isolation and small population against itself. It was a bold move, if it didn't work then the small force would be wiped out but who would expect him to do this?

They dropped down to the bottom of the cliff and seeing the carvings from close up, she noticed the channels inside used to drain the rain water away from the cliff face - the branches weren't just there for decoration. Mika heard a few soldiers swearing at the sight of the carved face of the fortress, the stone trees curling across the rock and the flashes of the coloured glass. It looked peaceful in the autumn day, the only thing that felt wrong was them being here.

"Animal." She remembered the cold eyes judging her on her heritage, despite the men in front having the same bloodlines. The only difference was a twist of fate that meant she could change her skin and they couldn't. As though the memory had woken the cat up again, it shifted inside and she shushed it. The forests called to her soul and the cat had become more restless the longer she stayed here. Alarmingly she'd found herself drifting off when the cat took over, a lethargy in her thoughts, accepting its dominance. She daren't talk about it, not to Jon who would worry or to Jehanne who would tell her to accept the beginning of the end.

The remaining Cassin swept the surrounding area of sentries. Now none remained outside the fortress. At some point someone would notice that they'd not come back. All they could do was wait.

The day crept on, this was worse in many ways than creeping through the forest. Everything depended on those men crawling through the ventilation shafts. She could almost see them in her mind's eye, dropping down to kill any who came across them by accident. They were relying on Jehanne's memories of being an adventurous child and Aurin's knowledge.

Rufus was close by, talking to his officers. Aurin came to sit next to her, he looked equally tense. They talked quietly for a while, watching the single road for any Cassai soldiers. The orders had been to stop anyone coming through.

He twisted a tendril of greenery around his fingers and Mika winced at the reduced movement in a couple of them. “I never told you this Mika, but I allowed myself to get caught by those peasants deliberately.”

“Why? I always had the idea you could slide through without being noticed.”

“I had my orders, I was supposed to kill Keira. I didn’t want to do it and I knew Dulcin was spreading rumours about spies, everything had become a lot harder than it should have been.” He hung his head. “I’ve got through that border easily many times.”

“Does Rufus know?”

“Yes, that’s why he wouldn’t let me out while I was in Ackbarr. He threatened the Cassin Mika, said if I didn’t do as he said, then he’d deal with them permanently. Dulcin knows about my connections with the Cassin, knows that I ride through the mountains with impunity. I don’t know if he knows that I report to them as well, that man winkles out information in ways I’ve never seen before.

“I panicked, I know how precarious everything is up there. All I could think of was that I’d be better off dead.” He took a deep breath, “Then I was rescued and found I didn’t want to die. Rufus gave me a new reason to live, new hope that the Cassin could survive.”

Mika wanted to hold his hand, to give him the sympathy he needed. “Do you think we can give that option to the others inside?” She nodded towards the cliff face.

“Maybe, they’re all terrified of him in there. No one knows what he’s going to do next. I’ve told Rufus that....” He broke off as a runner approached.

Mika and Aurin found themselves moving closer to hear what he had to say. The birdsong and trees made it hard, but she clearly heard him say that the engineers were in place and the river would begin flooding the tunnels in several hours. Mika looked at Rufus sharply, she'd only heard part of his plans, he'd kept everything very close to his chest. He'd listened to everything she and the others had said and this was the one thing that could drive the ruling elite out of their stronghold. Once it was released, the water would surge through the tunnels, gradually filling them.

The thought of the water slowly rising made her shiver. She'd heard the river was strong and at a far higher level and those stone doors only held back human invaders, not the insidious flow of black liquid. She came closer and asked, "Are you going to warn them?"

"No." Rufus' eyes were flat, "They come out with what they have. Once I have certain people under arrest then I'll send my soldiers in to get what I can. I intend this to be over as quickly as I can."

"Once the river has been sprung, it won't be easy to re-seal it back into its original flow. I read that it happened years ago and they lost a lot of people trying to sort it. The stone doesn't tolerate getting soaked, it eventually collapses once it gets too wet." Aurin's grin was wolfish, his self-pity gone.

"Once we have our hostages, I'll secure the main hall. The waters won't get that far up for a while." Mika closed her eyes, this was war. It was a cold comfort to remind herself that she wasn't fighting at the borders.

"We can stop the fighting quicker this way." Rufus was looking at her with sympathy, "Believe me, I don't want too much resentment here either, we need to rule afterwards and this is the best way to do it. We may be able to divert the flow back once we're in and away from certain areas but I'm not promising anything."

She swallowed, "How are they going to know that we've won?"

"I'm going to have Dulcen nailed to the front door." Aurin's fists were clenched. "He'll never subject anyone to what happened to me again. We've a chance to make this straight, for everyone."

Mika hoped he was right. There had been a break in the tree canopy close to the top of the cliff and she'd seen the dark clouds gathering overhead. Once those hit the mountains then it would rain hard, and swell the rivers and streams. Several of those rivers would run underground and flow past Dubari. How much of difference would it make to the threatened flooding of the tunnels, and what of the libraries?

Rufus rubbed a hand through his sweaty hair, making the short crop stand up, "My only problem here is that I don't trust Jehanne entirely any more, she's changed over the last few months."

"She's hanging on with everything she has." Aurin said softly, "She won't last much longer."

"I don't know if putting the Cassin in charge is right if they degenerate like this. She's fixating on one thing only and it's not what we agreed on."

Aurin said, "Jehanne would have gone months ago without this to concentrate on. Hal's been gone for several years now, he only reacts if something upsets her."

Mika shook her head, uneasy at their worries. It was too much to deal with, she could only think about what was now and that was waiting for Dubari to realise that their sentries hadn't come back on time or for the flooding to be noticed.

She moved away as she and Aurin were relieved of their duty and she found a tree to lean against. The men were strung out around the clearings taking it in turns to sleep, the Cassin loping between the groups. Between the two parties no one could get through without them knowing. Rufus had turned Dubari's strength into a weakness. There was only one main way out of the fortress. The ventilation shafts would be blocked after the sappers had come back up. The bird song and sunlight on the leaves felt unreal at the thought of the water rising.

The soldiers slept as experienced campaigners and Mika was jealous. Jon was in another group, Medici couldn't be in the same – they were too important. She held her hands over her mouth and breathed through them, fighting her panic. A nudge on her thigh and Stafa leaned against her. Her fingers sank through his ruff and she pulled him close as she sat against the tree, her eyes fixed on the entrance.

She sank into a doze, allowing the cat to take over and ignoring her worry about being like Jehanne. The sun had moved overhead, their own soldiers stirred and some lazily drinking from their flasks. Gnats buzzed and Stafa snapped at one. The movement shocked her into noticing a stirring at the entrance. She shifted and Risone swung his head to look as she motioned. Some riders appeared - they'd be allowed to leave sight of the entrance but no further.

She watched as they mounted and rode down the track, most of them were as sandy-haired as she was. Mika found herself counting the seconds away and straining her ears. There was little to be heard until a riderless horse burst back into the area in front of the entrance. It snorted, tossing its head as though unsure what to do next and then trotted back to the stables close to the cliff edge.

Risone remarked, “Well that’s fucked us, they’ll know we’re here now.”

There was definitely some consternation now, people were coming out and looking agitated. A group of lightly armed men were standing close to the entrance, peering around. She could see the crossbows they held and one was directing them to different areas, his movements calm and decisive. The soldiers next to her were carefully picking up weapons, those dozing having woken and moving back, away from the possible killing zone. There were so few of them, she couldn’t understand why Rufus hadn’t brought more people and sent them down the ventilation shafts. She loosened her own rapier and felt ill about using it.

The Cassai men marched out from under cover and Mika saw the signal, several flashes of light from a mirror. Bolts buzzed out from the trees in all directions. Lessons learnt indeed, the crossbows Rufus was using were heavier and had more distance than the repeater bows the Cassai used. Unable to use the cover to creep up and get close, the lighter, faster weapons were useless. No one made it back into the fortress. Silence reigned and the bodies lay in the darkening skies, there was a rumble overhead. Her eye caught a movement in the dark of the entrance and another single bolt flashed. A foot flopped out and stayed there. She had to suppress the urge to go and help.

A rustling behind them, one of the Cassin slid out of the undergrowth and speak to Risone. After a few muttered words he disappeared to speak to the next group. Risone spoke to a few of the men and they spread whatever the Cassin had said.

He came up to her, “The engineers have done their job and are out.”

“So it’s just a matter of waiting?”

Risone nodded, “The ones that got out say it won’t be diverted easily, it’s flooding far faster than they expected.” At her look he said, “Yes, we lost a few men to the water. The Cassai caught some of them before they got back into the shafts as well. The Cassai will have lost a lot more.”

“So they know they’re under attack.” It wasn’t a question.

“We just have to hold out until more men come.” They were dead otherwise and Keira would likely die in Ackbarr as well. The dukes wouldn’t care about the daring plan, they would only see the failure. Her father had only just kept his place due to the other military campaigns he’d succeeded with.

“I don’t see why we couldn’t have gone in there with more soldiers.”

Risone snorted, “Fight in there? Look, I don’t know about the Commander’s plans but I do know I don’t want to be fighting in the dark. Trust Rufus.” He slapped her shoulder in comradeship. A fat drop of rain splatting onto a leaf distracted her. “And it’s raining.” His voice filled with disgust. “I hate fighting in the rain.”

Mika smiled, despite herself. “It won’t last long and it’ll dry out quickly at this time of the year. We tend to have short frequent showers, it keeps the forest green. It’ll be far worse up in the mountains.”

He grunted, “And it’ll feed the rivers?”

“Yes.” Her voice was softer.

“Good, it’ll get this shit sorted faster then.”

They spent several days parrying sorties made by the Cassai. The stained glass windows were broken so bolts could be fired from a greater height in an attempt to catch any unwary Ackbarr soldier. The Cassai had tried sneaking out at night to get to the road and also attempted climbing the cliff. They had no chance against the Cassin. They were hunted down by them in their cat forms, their sensitive eyes and noses picking up any trails left. Mika stayed away from the Cassin after hearing some of the stories.

Bodies had piled up both on the road leading up to the fortress and also at the entrance. Any that could be dragged away, were. There was no way they could risk burning the bodies at the moment, smoke would signal quicker than the absence of riders that there was a problem to other settlements. It was a game of bluff and double bluff, neither side quite knowing what was going on with the other.

Messengers were constantly going to and fro. Everyone kept half an eye on Rufus, Mika was impressed by her friend's coolness in this situation. He laughed and joked with his men and she could see why he was considered such a good leader, not everything was purely down to his prowess with weapons.

The only person he became impatient with was Jehanne. Her passiveness with Hal frustrated him. Both Aurin and Mika stayed close by as he tried to grill her further, "You said the tunnels were at a lower level – yes?" Jehanne didn't answer, her eyes were unfocussed and Hal growled, softly.

Aurin spoke up, "All the tunnels out start at a far lower level. Dubari is high, that ridge that forms the cliff behind it, they couldn't tunnel further that way due to the rivers. All the tunnels come this way."

"You think they'll be flooded by now?" Rufus chewed a thumb nail. Mika suddenly realised what Rufus had been doing with releasing the river. She swore as she remembered her history, last time the Cassai had used the tunnels to pop up and ambush

Ackbarr soldiers. Rufus was counting on penning the Cassai nobility into Dubari using the river.

Aurin nodded, "At the very least they'll be hard to get to. Once the tunnel entrance close to Dunbarin is impassable then the entrances will definitely be blocked."

"I've got several Cassin watching that one, they say it's smelling very damp in there and it's likely to be flooded."

"Do you want me to sneak in and check?"

"No, we'll save that for later."

The days stretched to a week. The rain fell harder every day, the promise of autumn in the crisper air in the mornings. She could almost taste it and despaired at having to be here. Jon shared her distaste but helped with any wounded. Mika expected proper re-enforcements to arrive at any point. Those Cassai killed trying to get to Dubari had been little more than normal traffic. Maybe the Ackbarr ships at Dunbarin had kept everyone else too occupied to notice. She'd heard snatches from the Cassin keeping Rufus abreast of the situation there.

The harbour was now free, their ships having pulled the scuttled Cassai boats to pieces. They were still blockading the ports, teasing the Cassai into sending their own ships out. Mika shook her head, she was sure that at some point someone would notice the lack of information coming out of Dubari and make the logical conclusion. They couldn't last much longer.

She was with Rufus when a young Cassin came over, breathless and exhausted. "It's not working on the border, the Cassai army is turning back. They must have heard something."

Rufus swore, this was not the news he wanted to hear. Dunbarin had been kept busy and the Cassai army should have been distracted by the fortress in the mountain pass. He nodded, his eyes cold, “We’ve got four days to get in there before we die. Send the signal for the ships to stop messing about, I want all the troops on shore.”

Chapter 10

There was a shout on the road, a frantic mirror signalling and Mika found herself in the middle of a pitched battle. The Cassin leapt, spooking the horses as they changed mid leap. Bolts flew, buzzing to take down the outriders. Dunbarin had sent a sizeable force to find out what was happening. No time to wonder how they'd realised, Mika flicked her rapier across the face of another soldier, each of them snarling in concentration. The riderless horses carried on in fright, bursting into the clearing before the fortress.

She couldn't think about having to kill her countrymen, nothing mattered apart from staying alive. The green piece of material tied around her head marked her as different to those fighting, a simple trigger to those who would kill anyone with Cassai features in their frenzy. Despite her cat disliking the slaughter, it marked its victims and stalked them, picking off those besieged by the heavier soldiers.

As the bodies piled up, with the riderless horses snorting and confusing the fighting, she came to a halt and became aware of other noises in the clearing. Dubari had realised reinforcements had arrived and had mounted an attack from the other side. Covered by a rain of poisoned arrows, their soldiers had advanced out of the fortress and were making their way to the road. Mika turned, her body coated in blood from a surgery she'd not wished to do.

"Hold fast, we've sorted one pack of dogs out, now for the next." Risone's voice was calm.

They melted into the forest and left the bodies into the road. Their own bowmen decimated the soldiers running towards the road, the makeshift shields barely more than planks of wood scavenged from furniture. Mika hated this, her countrymen had never needed to protect themselves from others using crossbow bolts, they'd never been pinned down like this. Fully half of them were cut down before they even made the lifeline to Dunbarin.

Risone called out to them, "Remember orders, if we can get one alive then do so."

The men were quickly swamped and a single man surrounded. Mika was close enough to see the terror in his eyes and the frantic struggling as his hands were forced behind his back by sheer numbers. Rufus was summoned, he spoke with the prisoner briefly with Aurin translating and he was shown the bodies on the forest track. Now the fight was over, she could see that he wasn't much older than her sons and how his body shook despite not being able to hear what Rufus said to him.

"Poor kid." Risone was stood next to her. "No one thinks any less of him."

"Hmm?" The cat was disgusted by the slaughter, this wasn't clean. The forests beckoned and she battened down her instinct to run away.

He nodded towards the young man. "He's not a soldier, just a lad who's been told to fight. He's terrified. He was brave to come out here."

"Maybe what's back there is worse."

Risone sighed, "Well hopefully we'll have the chance to cut that out. You know, the lads are getting the chance to know the Cassin and they're liking them. Nothing quite like fighting to force people to depend on each other."

Rufus was still talking with his hand on the boy's shoulder. He nodded to what he heard, tears streaming down his face. Rufus walked him to the edge of the clearing himself, and stuffed white rags into his clothing, talking all the time while he pointed out the Cassin standing next to Ackbarr soldiers. Mika wondered if this was the next twist in Rufus' plan. Unexpectedly, Rufus pulled the lad into an embrace, rubbing his hand through his hair and the lad straightened as he let him go.

"Fuck me if he hasn't done it again." Mika looked at Risone and he nodded at Rufus. "That's why the men would follow him to hell and back and he's got that lad as well now. Let's hope he can talk to the others inside and persuade them."

The lad's hands were untied and Rufus sent him out into the clearing with another clap on his back. He walked into the open space with the rags lifting in the breeze and his hands up, one slow step at a time. Mika could feel how everyone was watching him with her, waiting to see what would happen. When he was within hailing distance, he stopped and shouted. Risone looked at her for a translation.

"He's saying he's been shown the army from Ackbarr and was left alive to tell them about what he's seen. That he's spoken to the Commander." She could hear the desperation in his voice and was aware of others coming closer to hear what she said.

"That is one brave lad."

There was no answer from the black holes in the carved cliff. He began walking again, slower this time, still shouting. Mika continued translating despite the worry building. "He says he needs to speak to Dulcin about what he's seen. That they've no chance of soldiers getting through." She strained to hear now.

The lad crumpled and fell to his knees with a cry. It happened so quickly she didn't see, it must have been a crossbow bolt. Another hit and he slumped onto the floor. A shiver went through Mika at the murmur from the men watching. Their eyes were flicking from the prone figure to their Commander, one word from him and they'd charge and to hell with the consequences.

Rufus bowed his head, his fists clenched. "Not now." They saw the flames in his eyes as he turned and said, "When the time's right. Not now…"

Aurin, Mika and Jon sprawled together, the two men uncaring that they were either side of the woman they both wanted. Stafa rested between her straddled legs, his paws underneath, his head on top. The men around them rested in similar positions with their comrades, taking comfort that they were living amongst the death they had generated.

They had two and a half days before the outriders and scouts from the returning Cassai army arrived and the main section of it wouldn't be far behind. It would soon be obvious that there were only a few of them surrounding the fortress and they would be swamped. Rufus walked through the exhausted groups, covered in blood and talking to the men, encouraging them. Mika saw the strength of his charisma as the men straightened in his presence, none of them wanting to be the one to let him down. Those who could, rested. Taking in it in shifts, the rest watched the fortress, road and forest for signs of movement.

The next ten hours were the worst, waiting for something to happen. They stayed out of sight of the entrance, the Cassin stalking any who tried to creep up on them with poisoned arrows. They had a hard glee about them, finally righting the wrongs of grandparents they had never known.

Mika and Jon dealt with injuries and helped to strip any bodies of useful equipment. The cat was very close to the surface, noting every twitch, every leaf flutter. She didn't know if it was the killing or the presence of the Cassin. She worried about her sons, especially once she'd heard they were over at Dunbarin. A tired gratefulness that they weren't involved in the killing here filled her, she didn't want them with blood on their hands.

Jon constantly stayed close to her, talking about nothing in particular. Had he sensed her difficulties? He'd known her for so long it was hard to keep anything from him. She longed to be held by him and was constrained by the men around them.

A movement behind and someone touched her shoulder. Mika crept back to see what the matter was and saw Rufus grinning like a madman. His excitement was infectious, she found her lips curling up tiredly in response.

"We've done it." He slapped her on the back, his voice was low and vicious.

"Done what?"

"Dunbarin is ours, a section will be coming out to help in the next half day." Mika allowed herself to sag in relief. They finally had a chance against the oncoming Cassai army. Reports had been flooding in from the Cassin keeping watch on their progress. If nothing else then they could retreat to Dunbarin. She gritted her teeth against such a thought, if they allowed the army to push them from here then they'd never get back to this position.

"More of our soldiers will be coming after the initial few, we're going to be fine. They know we've got Dubari pinned down." Until the Cassai arrived, then they'd be the ones to be pinned between two forces. "Just a little longer now." He stopped himself, "You may want to see the runners who brought the message." He jerked his head to where they kept their supplies and Mika went, not knowing what he meant.

She found Rey and Deon near one of the supply piles. Her heart leapt for a moment and then crashed as she noticed Rey's arm around his twin and Kaylan sprawled over his lap. Deon had a blanket over his shoulders and was staring into the ground, his face white. She rushed over, worrying that he'd been hurt. Kaylan got up off Deon's legs and he curled up into her arms, burying his head into her shoulder like a much younger child.

Tucked away in the bushes away from the other men, Mika could be what she was – a woman capable of giving comfort to her child, even if he didn't know it. She shushed him as sobs heaved his body, stroking back his hair and marvelling at the fact that this young man had come out of her own body.

At last he pulled away slightly although not enough to break the contact. "I killed him," was all he said and he crumpled again.

Rey said quietly, "Deon saw him before I did, Papa wasn't there then. He took him down." He bit his lip and her heart plummeted. Mika pulled Deon close again and held him as she'd never held one of her children before, tightly and wishing she could take the memory away. She'd never wanted either of them to go through what she had.

"I wish I could be like Papa, he doesn't care if he kills or not." The words were low and muttered. "I wish I could change and never change back."

"Don't say that, I've missed my brother for so many years. You don't want Rey to go through what I did." She nearly shook him, the sharpness of her anger surprising her. "I loved my brother, as much as you two love each other and now he's gone completely."

"But I killed that man." Deon choked, "His blood was all over my hands and he looked at me when he was dying as though he couldn't believe it was happening. Hunting is different, it's clean, not like this."

"I know, but you did it to help keep people safe. We've a chance to stop this before too many other people get hurt." Mika daren't say to him that this was the reason why she hadn't wanted him to come along. She'd tried, it hadn't worked. She took a deep breath, "I always found, before I stopped being able to change that is, that allowing the cat to take me away helped. I don't know why, it just did."

He twisted in her arms. "I don't want to forget, forgetting won't help."

"I didn't say forget, just let the cat take you away for a bit." She rocked him, knowing it was unlikely she'd ever hold him like this again. He buried his head in her shoulder for a moment, pressing his face hard against her and then stood, walking into the bushes without saying anything. Rey watched, wide eyed. Mika shoved at Kaylan with her foot, "Go with him."

The large grey cat flowed after her son and she looked at his twin brother.

"I wish it had been me." Rey shook his head, "Not that I want to have killed someone but I deal with things differently. Deon cares."

"So do you but yes, you're right." She held out an arm, wanting the chance to hold her other son. "Need a hug as well from your ancient aunt?" She saw the slight hesitation and braced herself for rejection. The surprise she felt when he slid over and carefully slung an arm over her shoulders delighted her.

"I'll give you one instead." He gave a shy smile, "I am bigger than you now."

She let herself relax for a moment, Rey had never been demonstrative. Despite the worry she felt over his brother, the hug relaxed her in a way she'd not been able to in the last few weeks. Mika patted his leg, wanting to distract him, "Let's go and find Jon, get him to tell you about the fun he's been having with that Weaven sapling."

Rey laughed, "How many times has it caught him?"

"Too many. The bloody thing keeps sliding out of the cage he made, it nearly got into the gutters on the roof once when he'd left it too long…"

Jon received them in delight, keeping his concern quiet over Deon's absence and then his subsequent return. Deon had red eyes and he kept his arm tightly around Kaylan. Mika worried for him, she offered to talk to him out of earshot of the rest of the men but he shook his head at her. Rey sat on the other side of Kaylan, his arm intertwined and gripping his brother's just as tightly. Jon told them stories softly, entertaining the soldiers around them as well as the boys. Gradually Deon relaxed and fell asleep, his features looking younger with the tear streaks down them. Mika caught some of the soldiers giving him sympathetic looks, strange on their hard faces. She guessed they had gone through similar at some point.

As the night progressed, more and more soldiers arrived from Dunbarin. Mika roused briefly at each group joining them. There was the soft murmur of men talking quietly in the forest night, relieving those standing guard and finding their own sleeping places.

That morning she woke to see many strange faces and bodies close by. She automatically looked for her sons and found them gone. A pang, they'd always been early risers. Kaylan was gone as well, he'd likely be with them – they'd be safe.

A rough voice asked, "You're the Cassai Medici?" She could see the look in his eye as he asked, wondering why she could betray her own country.

"Cassin," she replied. The name still felt strange to her despite being correct. She could change, she was Cassin, not Cassai. "I am considered an animal here." He nodded doubtfully and held out his arm.

Mika pulled her bag close and began unwrapping the rough bandage to find a knife wound. "Hang on, I'll stitch this for you. Have we had many re-enforcements?" She cleaned it quickly.

A grin split his face, showing black teeth. "Five hundred men, more ammunition and supplies. We've stopped any rebellion in the city." He paused, considering. "Pretty little place with all those trees and carvings. Wouldn't mind settling down there. Find myself a nice white haired wife and a tavern to run." He laughed, "If they've forgiven us by the time I retire."

She smiled back, he was a career soldier, running a tavern with a willing wife was probably the pinnacle of his ambition. "You've heard about the army approaching us from the border?"

"Aye, we'll give them a hard time." A low mutter alerted them to another sortie from the fortress. Despite her grasping his arm to begin stitching, he hefted his crossbow and then relaxed when he saw it wasn't needed. He winced at the sting from her needle and nodded towards the entrance, "You'd have thought they would have prepared better for this."

"Arrogance." Mika hated to say this. "Last time Ackbarr didn't get this far and we've flooded the lower tunnels."

He sucked his teeth thoughtfully, "Never a good thing to assume no one can get at you. I suppose the tavern thing here wouldn't be a good idea – I'd have to hide all the knives from the missus."

There were several more attempts to get out that day. Rufus paced, swearing at the delay and Mika watched, equally concerned. Even with the extra troops, it was going to be hard to hold back the Cassai army heading towards them. They were in their own land and their presence would give hope to those in the Dubari fortress. They now only had a day or so before the outriders and scouts would reach them. Mika could see Rufus working out ways of sending his own army to meet them.

A soldier called Rufus over, he was pointing at the entrance. At first Mika couldn't work out what it was, then she saw the darker stain coming out of the cave mouth. "That shouldn't be happening so fast."

Rufus rubbed his chin, "I can't send any engineers back in, they'd get caught and they aren't soldiers." He went off to talk to several while Mika stared at the steady trickle. Water expanding through the caves, blocking off rooms, trapping the occupants. The slow cold rise, there wouldn't be any escape. Rufus' face was vicious when he came back.

"The sappers reckon they disturbed more than just the single river. It's been throwing it down in the mountains as well. According to Aurin, it normally backs right up through the tunnels this time of year. They have overflows to deal with it but having this new outlet, the water's taking the easier way which must be right through Dubari."

"And you don't think they know about their army coming back?"

He clenched his fist, "I can practically guarantee it. I need to speak to the men, those inside are going to be feeling the pressure."

Mika returned to staring at the entrance. It would either be an all-out fight or it would be surrender. She could almost feel the wavering between the two options and remembered Dulcin's face and knew he wouldn't give up.

Several hours later there was a flurry of motion at the entrance. All crossbows were pointed at the tall figure coming out with his hands raised above his head. His hair was as sandy as hers, as dark as the Cassin.

The man was on his own, his head held arrogantly, the toss suggesting he didn't feel he was surrendering despite his hands spread far apart. She almost snorted, her kinsmen had been brought up to think themselves superior. Part of the elite and yet not able to change, that took a twisted mindset. Despite her misgivings, she had to admit that it had taken some courage to come out first.

He stopped in the middle of the clearing and shouted in broken Ackbarri that he was unarmed. Mika worked her way round to where Rufus stood, a short way back from the beginning of the trees and out of range. He touched a soldier's shoulder and he went to the edge to answer. The Cassai walked up to him and had his hands tied behind his back.

"They are surrendering, the men will come out one at a time." There was a flash of triumph in the man's face as he reported to Rufus. One by one they came, splashing through the water pouring out of the entrance to be tied up and led to a small clearing guarded by soldiers. She looked and didn't see Dulcin or Phineas, somehow she wasn't surprised. Mika caught Rufus' arm and he nodded at her.

"He's holed himself up there, this lot aren't important anymore."

"They are Rufus, they are still royal family." More were coming out, this time their hair was paler, rather than sandy. These would be servants, librarians and the like. They were taken to a different area.

"Check them over," Jon said. "It's not so difficult to bleach hair."

"I want you helping." Jon nodded at Rufus' command and left.

Rufus paced in front of the group of Cassai men as Mika watched, his arrogance matched theirs. She could now see how close they appeared to be to the Cassin. Some of they looked a step away from changing, although she knew they'd have been extensively tested to make sure they couldn't. She shuddered, she'd heard that those that had succumbed had left for Phineas' laboratory.

He said, "This is going to be simple. Swear your allegiance to Ackbarr and you can live." Aurin translated his words into Cassai.

There weren't many in the group, about forty or so and a mix of ages, the youngest looked about fourteen and no women or children had come out. She wondered where they were, the men had refused to speak of anything. Her eye was caught by the youngest lad, he looked as though he might start crying at any moment. She braced herself knowing she couldn't get involved in this. These nobles were the key, if they swore allegiance then Cassai would be Ackbarr's.

One man, several years older tossed his head, "Fuck that."

"Fine." Rufus jerked his head and two guards pulled him out from the group. A rope was thrown over a branch and he was hung in short order. Mika felt sick, Rufus had planned this. No mercy to anyone who didn't swear. Big tears were running down the boy's face and his shoulders were shaking. None of the group touched him, held in the moment and Rufus' gaze as he stared them down. They wouldn't be used to this, they'd been used to having people obey them. The privileges of leading the life they'd had. Could they bend their heads to a foreign power?

"Do I need to call you out one by one?" Rufus let the challenge hang in the air between them. He waited and then huffed, ready to make his next order.

"Wait, don't be scared. It's easy."

A movement to the side. Mika started as she saw Deon walking confidently up to Rufus. He turned to the group, speaking in Cassai. Aurin swiftly translated his words as he spoke to Rufus. "I am Deon Leafen." He used the Cassai custom of naming himself after the place he'd been brought up. Mika saw Rey on the outskirts of the clearing, his face in shock.

"You are a half breed." It was said scornfully by one of the older men.

He raised his chin, "I am Cassin although I was brought up Cassai. I would like to swear to Ackbarr."

Rufus blinked and recovered swiftly, "Of course, repeat these words after me." He talked Deon through the ritual and paused for a moment as Deon knelt in front of him and then tapped him on the shoulder in acknowledgement of his vow. He turned the youth around to face the group, his hands on his shoulders.

Deon looked at the boy only a couple of years younger than himself and held a hand out, "It's easy." The boy looked scared and another man bristled, opening his mouth to say something.

"Are you offering to swear?" Rufus got in before him and his mouth hung open, caught. Deon walked up to the boy, catching his arm and the others shifted slightly to leave a gap around him.

"What's your name?"

The boy shook his head, tears still running down his face. He muttered, "They'll kill them if I do." The low tone still carried through the clearing.

Mika was impressed, Deon didn't even blink, "What do you mean?" The boy froze, shocked at his audacity and unable to answer. "We may be able to help. Are you talking about your mother or sisters?" He'd obviously cottoned onto the fact that there were no women or children in the group. The boy nodded, miserable. "Are they in the tunnels?" Another slight nod, the shoulders cringing from the displeasure of the other men. "What if we got them out? What then?" A dreadful hope sprang up in the boy's eyes, a shifting from some of the others. She could tell some of them wouldn't find the idea of a different allegiance difficult if the womenfolk were safe.

"If you tell me, then we will do what we can."

"It's a fucking trap, they'll die and so will you." This burst out from the man Rufus had challenged. "Draven there," He nodded at the swinging corpse in the tree. "He had two children inside and his wife." Mika felt sick again.

"Why did you come out then?"

The man snorted, "We were given a choice, we could come out here and take our chances or watch our wives and children die." There were murmurs from the other men.

It was a trap, Mika had known Dulcin wouldn't give in easily. She wondered what he had planned, his face rose in her mind's eye again, the lines deep around his mouth and the cold eyes. She asked, "What about Phineas?"

"He's backing Dulcin." This was muttered. These men were proud, brought low by their love for family members.

"Do you know what he's got planned?"

A shifting amongst them and the boy said, "He's got changers there. He'll set them on anyone who tries to get at him."

Rufus nodded sharply, his face shuttered while he thought. He raised his head, "Settle them down for the moment. No mistreating them while I decide what to do." He motioned to Mika to follow him as he walked away.

Chapter 11

Mika followed the tall Cassin through the undergrowth, several others were following behind her. Jon was back at the camp with the twins, Rufus had refused to allow him to come. His position as Medici made him valuable and they already had her going with the group. Jon hadn't been happy but hadn't questioned his orders.

Her worry expanded, Aurin had been sent in through the ventilation shafts, and hadn't come back yet. Rufus had been using Rey and Deon to translate instead. She'd seen his arm twitch when one Cassai had spat and muttered about the half breeds. He knew they were her sons and had seen Aurin's worth in the last few months and had appreciated both his consistency and his willingness to help in any way he could. Everyone knew there was no way Aurin would have gone back to Dulcin willingly.

Seeing Aurin with his hair bleached before he'd left had made her catch her breath, remembering those few nights in Dunbarin. He'd caught her reaction and had grinned, not allowed any further reaction around the men. He'd dressed like a Cassai servant, the idea had been to open an air shaft and blend in with any servants left and find out the situation.

He'd not come back yet so Rufus had agreed to Jehanne's other suggestion to send Cassin in. With so little time before the Cassai army arrived, he'd not had much choice. Much to Mika's misgivings, Jehanne was coming but thankfully leaving Hal.

Mika dropped back to speak to her. "Are you alright?"

Jehanne twisted, a sinuous shiver as she spotted something move in the undergrowth. Mika had to stop herself from doing the same and refused to think of how little time either of them must have left. Jehanne said, "I have to go in, to see for myself."

Mika could see the effort it was taking for her to get the words out. It wouldn't be long before she'd only be echoing anything like Kaylan. "We need to get the women and children out." Jehanne nodded, her eyes glazing over. The rest of the Cassin ignored Jehanne's behaviour, the decline was an accepted normality to them. She tried again, "Hal's not coping, you'll need to take him away soon." Hal had been snarling at the soldiers, Jehanne was only just holding him back while trying to stay human.

"I must get inside, they are being held."

Mika gave up and concentrated on climbing the steep path instead. A squat chimney rose, its top capped by a large stone. All the ventilation shafts were either collapsed or capped and patrolled to make sure they weren't disturbed by the occupants within. A simple pulley system was ready and waiting to pull the stone up. Mika shivered, it would be stuffy down there, the only air would be from the small broken windows in the cliff.

She watched as the first man pulled himself up and dropped down the shaft. Her stomach was churning, she'd not done much of the fighting up to this point, she'd mostly been involved in patching people up. A couple more men disappeared and then it was her turn. The shaft was as tight as she remembered, she felt for the grooves and slid until she felt the man catch her swinging feet to guide them. She muffled a squeal and jumped at the reassuring pat in return.

"You're fine lady." She had a brief surprise at his comment and then gave a grateful chuckle - she didn't need to pretend here, they knew what she was. Mika moved along the narrow tunnel on hands and knees, taking the clothes given her by the changer in front. She stuffed them into the bag she held and almost felt the change happen, the atmosphere becoming more alert. Once they were all down, they followed the cat's nose in front, guiding them until they slid down another shaft to land in a room.

The lanterns were lit, showing the honey coloured stone enclosing them. It felt like a tomb now, the stuffy air barely circulating. Mika loosened her rapier and tried not to think about using it in cold blood. There were ten of them. Half of them stripped and changed, the other half stayed human to give a different perspective. Mika glanced at Jehanne and saw her sway, she linked hands with her and Jehanne smiled a little at the contact.

They crept along the corridors, led by the cats. The flicking of an eye and whisker twitch meant everything here. Those human shaped kept conversation to a minimum, ears straining for any clue beyond the lantern light. Mika could almost feel herself sinking into a dream with the cat taking over, walking through the stone corridors, her hand clasped around Jehanne's. The tunnels caught echoes in a strange way, picking up the scuff of a foot and yet dampening other sounds.

They went down at every junction, Mika saw the carvings for the library and wondered if the books had been moved to a higher level. She mourned the death of this place, the hundreds of years it had been inhabited even if it had been taken over by those maddened by power in more recent times. A tension swept over the party, Mika found herself on high alert, stepping carefully and tilting her head to catch any sound.

"We're being watched." The mutter came from one of those in human form.

Mika asked, "Who by?" and got no response other than a shrug. "Why aren't they doing anything?"

"We're going where they want us to go." There couldn't be many left in the complex, those considered Cassai royalty were as scarce as the Cassin themselves and most of the men had been forced out. She could see the cats in front lifting their heads to sniff.

Someone whispered, "I can smell fear."

Mika barely needed the translation, her own cat pushing through with the others around them. "Who do you think it is?"

A cat rippled into his human form, "Women and children, they are frightened." He bared his teeth. "Follow."

She was worried, Dulcin would know of the Cassin's strong family ties and any Cassai who were here would be related close enough to trigger it. There was nothing she could do, they had to get them out to hold the men who'd surrendered and there was no way the Cassin would leave them here now. She kept walking, on edge and following the cats in the lead.

The smell grew stronger until she could almost taste it. There was a soft murmuring close by and the wail of a child shushed. Mika's anger grew and she struggled to keep the cat down. The damp coolness of water was also apparent, they weren't far from the rising flood.

The leading cats stopped at the corner and changed, reaching for the clothes passed to them by their companions. Mika still held Jehanne's hand, she was mouthing things in a dreamworld. Mika shook her, Jehanne focussed briefly and said, "We must save them."

Fed up, Mika dropped her hand, she was lost in the past and they had to deal with the present. The murmurs had grown louder at the light and Mika heard the lead Cassin swear as he rounded the corner. In the light, black bars blocked the way through and women and children were huddled behind them. Beyond was the slow rise of flood water, lapping closer every second.

Mika saw them flinch at the half naked Cassin and shoved her way to the front. She inspected the bars, they'd been pulled into place by chains and then pins had been wedged into the yellow rock. It would be a simple matter to lever them out from their side and push the gate towards the prisoners. She ordered a couple of the men to start knocking the pins out while she tried speaking to the women.

"Why were you left here?"

An older woman replied, "They said we had to stay behind the bars for our safety and then the water started rising."

"Who and safety from what?"

"Our men brought us here, I believe they were ordered to. They said the cats that would be hunting in the corridors."

"You don't need to worry about cats," one of the Cassin snorted. "There's only us here."

"Have you any injuries?"

"No, we're just cold and hungry."

Mika backed away to allow the iron bars be pulled out of the way and then gestured to the women and children to come out. They filed out slowly, peering at the dark beyond the lanternlight. There weren't many of them, most of the servants were men and had come out earlier. Mika hadn't seen any women when she'd come to Dubari before, and she felt her blood begin to boil, they'd been locked up like her mother. She forced herself to calm down, losing her temper wouldn't help anyone.

Several women were attempting to pick someone up, Mika went to see as they appeared to be hurt despite what the woman had said. She crouched, holding the lantern up and saw an older man, his hair spilling over his face. He looked half-starved and ill. Mika touched his shoulder and he muttered something.

One of the women asked, "Can we get him out as well?" Mika nodded and called to a Cassin who slung the man over his shoulder with a grunt. Not the most comfortable way of getting him out but they didn't have that luxury. All her nerves were twitching and she could see the others felt the same.

They began walking up the slope, Jehanne was at the front, still in her dream and with her eyes glazed. "Save the kittens," she murmured as Mika caught up.

"Jehanne, can you lead us to the shaft? The others need to check the tunnels we go past."

She nodded and turned, whispering, "They kept changing, bolts hitting them, changing." Mika despaired, she was re-living her past.

"Jehanne, I need you to…" She sniffed, what was that smell? Smoke in the tunnels? They had no ventilation here apart from the windows - her blood went cold – and the chimney they'd opened. Were they trying to smoke them out? Asphyxiate them? "Keep moving."

She passed the whisper on fiercely, pushing at the women to move faster. The cat stirred underneath, stretching out paws and wanting to be let out. She shook her head at it, not now - later. They passed more junctions, always moving upwards. Mika daren't think how they'd get the women up the shafts, let alone the wounded man. She wondered who he was and why he'd been left instead of being taken out.

Soft noises on the edge of her hearing bothered her, she shook her head again and noticed the other Cassin doing the same. The cat inside batted at her insistently, wanting her attention. Mika sniffed again and froze, a woman bumping into her from behind. She recognised that smell, it drifted through the tunnels and past fifteen years. She knew why the other Cassin were shaking their heads and why the women had been warned to stay behind the bars. The hatred in a young man's eyes as he waved a handful of herbs at her beyond the bars, trying to force the change. The cats they had to worry about were the ones they carried within themselves. The Cassai were using them against their selves.

Mika swore loudly, "Keep moving, and cover your faces. They're using herbs to make us change." She pushed her way to the front of the group, hustling them along as she did. The tunnels all looked the same to her, she couldn't use her nose like the cats leading them could. She swore further, that irritation she felt with the noise, was it affecting the cats?

Jehanne was in front, walking in her dream. The cat she was following was shaking its head, its ears akimbo from the half heard noise. "Jehanne, when you were taken from here, how did you get out?" Jehanne turned to her and Mika saw how diffused her eyes were in the dim light.

"Out." She repeated sleepily.

"Yes, out. You couldn't have taken the babies and children through the shafts, how did you get out?" Why hadn't they realised this? There was no space to get them up the ventilation shafts, had they really just walked out of the main entrance, or even through the old tunnels that were now flooded?

"Kittens…" Jehanne said softly. "I was just a kitten, curious, walking in front."

"Like now Jehanne, how did you get out?"

"A long tunnel, we walked, they didn't know about it."

"Were you chased? How did you get out Jehanne?" She pinched Jehanne's arm, hoping to pull her back to some form of consciousness.

A growl to the side and Mika heard a woman muffle a squeal. The cat in front turned lambent eyes on them and Mika suppressed her own cat wanting to respond. She used every trick, pleading and begging for it not to manifest itself. The noise was getting louder, lodging itself in her brain. They meant for the Cassin to kill the women and children, they'd display the bodies afterwards. The men would rebel, no chance of surrender. She talked to her own cat, reminding it of their time in the cage and how it was time to hide. It didn't want to know this time, it snarled inside wanting to fight. Almost desperate she said, "The kittens Jehanne, how do we get the kittens out."

"Books on shelves, so many books. I wanted to stop and touch them." Jehanne bowed her head, "We had to keep walking. There was a tunnel past the books."

"The library." By chance she glanced up and saw the marker. "Head that way, keep talking to those in front, we have to protect the kittens."

One of the women was struggling with a child, Mika took him and was reminded of a small pair of arms twining around her own neck in the cold and realised with a start that it must have been Tamar, years ago and thought how he'd cuddled up to her with no fear. The cat remembered, she could feel its mood changing, becoming more protective. Sleep, she suggested and the cat agreed, it walked around in a circle, curling up. She could almost feel how it tucked a paw over its ears and its nose into itself.

Mika buried her chin into the child's shoulder, tightened her arms and gave it to one of the men walking next to her. He was weaving, his eyes unfocussed but he straightened when given the child. The woman walked next to him, her eyes worried.

His change in stance gave her the clue to deal with the herbs, they had to use the protective instincts of the Cassin. Asking the women softly, she gave the younger children to the Cassin, telling them to hold and protect them. Several of them were weaving and yet they all curled their arms around the children, talking to them softly.

In the dark tunnels, the way to the library felt longer that it should. Those Cassin in cat form regularly turned to snuff the older children walking behind them. Mika told the women to keep reminding the children to touch them. It was a strange situation, the Cassin protecting the women and children who were in turn protecting them. None of the children minded the large faces pushing against them, they stroked the soft fur in delight.

The noises were drowned out by the women's whispers, the smoke by the children, she could only hope they could get out of here before one or the other failed. She was on edge every second, if one cat turned then it would be chaos, nothing would hold them. Mika held Jehanne's arm tight, keeping her with them.

Finally the entrance appeared with the large carving of a scroll over it and Mika sighed with relief. She asked someone to lead them to the cat carving, thankful that the women knew the library. All the books had been removed, Mika hoped to a safe place.

It was eery with the empty shelves looking down on them.

"They left a rope hanging from the shafts when they recused us. I touched it as I went past."

The archway appeared with the cat leaping over it. Jehanne reached out a hand and changed it into a cats paw, slotting her claws into the leaves and pulling. The door opened halfway and stopped as before.

"And what did you do next?" Mika took a lantern and shoved Jehanne through the door and into the room. They nearly tripped over the remains of the tapestry, it had been thrown back in without regard for its age.

"Here." The marks were hidden in the shadows behind where the tapestry had hung. Jehanne pulled and part of the case opened inwards. Fusty air blew out, making them shake their heads and Mika nearly laughed. All that time a door had been here, hidden by a disgusting hanging that no one would have wanted to touch.

"Come on, we need to get out." Mika pulled the first door shut behind them and waited for the last of the Cassin to slide through the second, cradling the child he carried like a talisman. She pulled the lever and it swung shut in her face. She'd have to hope no one would come looking for them, that they'd assume the Cassin would have turned on the women.

There was no time to look for anything to block the mechanism, they ran in the straight tunnel. No one cared about the noise being made, the Cassin stretching out their legs, the soft thud of feet and paws hitting the ground in front of the main group. It was full of cobwebs, but Mika could feel the breeze.

They stumbled out into the forest about half a mile from Rufus' camp. The entrance to the cats door was well hidden and Mika wondered if there were any more tunnels coming out whose entrances had been lost in history. They lay, panting the dark and the smoke out of head and lungs in the lush green.

"You are changers. Why did you help us?" The question came from one of the women as she took her child away from the Cassin holding him.

He shrugged, "I am Cassin and you are family. The children should be protected." He raised a hand to tug at his own dark blonde hair as though it were obvious.

The woman protested, "We are the royal family."

"What else do you think the royal family is?" He laughed and it left the woman speechless, cradling her child tightly.

"We're supposed to be animals according to Dulcin." Mika raised her own voice. "I've been called an animal by him but I'm also a Medici, I studied in Ackbarr and they accepted me there. What does that make me? Is your child an animal if he can change? Does that stop you caring about them?"

"It's a deformity…"

"It's natural. It happens." Mika was firm. If Rufus was successful and the Cassin came back, then Cassai was going to have to learn to deal with what happened and not shut it away.

"Who locked you up and who freed you?" Jehanne had come out of her trance. "We are not the animals."

"I have a child who was taken away several weeks ago. They all are after a certain age, regularly for the tests. Some don't come back." An older woman spoke up and a few others nodded.

"Did your child come back?" She shook her head at Mika's question. "Do you think they're still in there?"

"I don't know. Sometimes I hope she is, other times…" She bowed her head, defeated.

"We'll try and find them." An empty promise, she had no idea if Rufus would let them in again. She left several Cassin on guard at the entrance just in case and sent others to warn Rufus that they were coming back.

The woman at the front stopped in shock when she saw the first Ackbarr soldier, "Wait, I thought…"

Mika nodded, knowing that they'd not told them that they were working for Ackbarr. A brief shame rose and she squashed it, they'd not had the time to argue about that as well as the Cassin. "It'll be fine, really."

She watched as they had their wrists tied together gently, most of them were too dazed to resist and were brought into the main camp. A tiredness swept over her, most of the Cassin were sprawling against tree trunks. Jehanne had her arms wrapped around Hal, muttering to him and running her fingers through his fur. The motion mesmerised her and she jumped as Rufus spoke, "Well?"

"They were trying to use smoke to make us change and something audible. It gets into our heads." She shook her own. "We barely made it out. I used the Cassin instinct of wanting to protect the children to stop them. You need to send soldiers out to the cat door where we got out, just in case we're followed."

Mika was barely able to stand. A nudge on her thigh and a familiar hand, she leaned back into Jon's arm and he helped hold her up.

Rufus nodded, “I’ll sort things from here. Did you see Aurin?”

Mika yawned, her mind on her fingers running through Stafa’s ruff. “We didn’t see anyone but they knew we’d be coming. They wanted us to kill the women and children. I need to sleep.” Rufus nodded and clapped her on the shoulder as she stumbled with Jon’s help to a clear space and fell into blackness.

Chapter 12

Mika muttered to herself at the weight on her legs as she half woke and shoved Stafa off. She shifted them and swore at the pins and needles lancing through. Her exhaustion had gone, the forest air and sounds had cleared her head as though by magic. Her own cat was peering out and asking nicely. Later, she promised, she also wanted the chance to run again and feel the clean wildness rather than the tainted tunnels.

There were soldiers moving with little regard for staying quiet. Her mind was brought back to the women and children they'd rescued and she wondered what had happened to them. Deciding she couldn't go back to sleep, Mika pulled herself up and went to look for Rufus.

She was waylaid by Jon. "Mikon, you need to come with me." He sounded urgent, unlike his usual self.

"What is it? What's happening?"

"The Cassai nobility have sworn fealty to Ackbarr but you need to see someone." He gave the ground breaking news almost casually while she stretched and followed him.

"That's fabulous Jon…" Her voice trailed off as she saw the man in the blankets under a makeshift shelter. It was the man that had been trapped with the women in Dubari. She felt a shame rise at not having thought of him before and her brain instinctively went into Medici mode. She crouched down, looking over his bruises. He was an older man and his hair was white blonde, so not one of the nobility. He looked half-starved and dirty. Something made her look twice and her hand went over her mouth.

“Steady…” Jon warned her. “He’s woken a few times and I’ve fed him. He’s fine, just been maltreated over a period of time.”

“Papa…” Mika heard her voice crack. She’d always seen her father neatly dressed, his status demanded it. He looked diminished lying on the floor asleep. Part of her wanted him upright and awake, she squashed her feelings - he needed to sleep.

She sat with him while he slept, wondering where Kaylan was and if he would even recognise their father now. Jon touched her shoulder as he left to deal with the other wounded. She felt no need to hide the tears, every soldier here was wound tight and anything that would have been perceived as a weakness normally would be ignored here – they’d all proved themselves. Her mind drifted back through the years to the times when she’d seen her father away from his work at the compound. Even there he’d exuded a calm confidence, his hands capable of guiding a horse over steep passes and a mind few would willingly cross in debate.

Mika blinked and wiped her face across her sleeve, sniffing loudly. She jumped as she realised her father’s eyes were open. His lips formed her name and then he started coughing. He accepted the water bottle she offered, sipping gratefully.

“I never expected to see the trees again, or you.” His voice was a hoarse whisper.

“Papa.”

As if in response to her tears, the heavens opened. She helped her father up into a sitting position and they sheltered under the same cloak, him with his arm across her shoulders. It was strange to feel him so close after so many years. They jacked their feet up and watched the rain dripping through the leaves.

“What happened Papa? Have you been locked up all this time?”

He nodded and then shrugged, “Dulcin made one of his decisions. I’d seen it happen before although they’d never affected me. He ordered Petron to go out with me to Ackbarr, ostentatiously to learn. I now believe he had other plans.”

“He was thrown out of Ackbarr and then the sickness came.”

“Sickness?” Koren drew back to look her full in the face, frowning.

“The sleeping sickness, those from Ackbarr never had much immunity to it. We’ve had three years of suffering and people dying. The city, it’s a different place now.”

His arm tightened around her although his face showed little. “I wasn’t told although I was kept on house arrest to begin with, I had access to any book I asked for and treated courteously. I wasn’t allowed any information from the outside world so I spent my time reading through their books on the Cassin. You have an interesting background Mika.” His eyes were shadowed.

“It’s not just my background, it’s all of Cassai. Cassin can crop up anywhere, they’re just more prevalent in the royal family because we’re so inbred.”

“And Rufus has them helping him.” He murmured, “Our own sword held at our throat.”

“Cassai did worse to us father, so many people have died.”

“Us?” He smiled at her choice of words. “Yes, it would have had that effect. Those who trade with us tend to know about the sleeping sickness, any newcomers are dealt with and become immune quickly.”

Mika kept on, “When we rescued the women, one of them said he took the children and tested them. Sometimes they didn’t come back.”

“He would have been testing them to see if they changed. The same tests he made both your mother and I take.”

“Both of you?”

“He wanted to be sure. I didn’t recognise them at the time, I read about them when I was able to request books, I must have read everything there is to know about the Cassin. The tests were only mildly irritating to me however when he tried them out on your mother after she’d had you two, she reacted.”

“I couldn’t change when I was pregnant either.” She said it softly, not wanting anyone to hear over the noise of the rain. Her father hugged her tighter.

Jon came through the wet branches, wincing as one sprang back. He offered a bowl to Koren. “Sorry, it’s only stew.”

“Anything is gratefully received, thank you.” He sighed, “The terms of my imprisonment changed when the twins escaped and I was put into a far less congenial cell. I would like to think Dulcin had forgotten about me but that man never forgets anything.”

Mika let Koren move away a little while he ate, he cuddled the bowl as though he couldn’t quite believe he was holding it. The rain was coming to a close, the warmth rising from the ground as the sun burst through the clouds again. She couldn’t stop herself from asking, “I once asked you if you kept Mama locked up. It wasn’t you, it was on Dulcin’s orders wasn’t it.”

Koren bowed his head, “Yes.” He pulled it back up as several soldiers went by, talking excitedly. “What is happening?”

Jon said, “We have about a day and a half until the main Cassai army get here. The outriders aren’t far away.”

Her father’s gaze sharpened in his thin face, “What is Rufus intending to do about it? I was impressed by both him and Keira while I was ambassador.”

“I don’t know, I think he was hoping to get Dulcin out and negotiate their surrender.”

“That won’t happen, Dulcin will die in there first.” Koren sat still for a moment, his gaze turned inwards. “Help me up and take me to Rufus, I may be able to suggest a few things.”

Rufus was pacing in another clearing, the contrast between him and her father – Rufus was muscular and at the height of his power. He reminded Mika briefly of Lord Eldon as he flicked his gaze towards them. Koren was gaunt in comparison, the years of neglect had taken a toll on him, he took his arm from Jon’s shoulder and squared his own.

“My Lord Rufus.” Koren gave a brief dip of his head and managed to make it look like he wasn’t going to fall over. “I would like to thank you for releasing me.”

“Ambassador Koren, please, sit down.” Rufus was immediately all concern as he flicked a finger at an officer. They brought over a wine skin and several blankets. “My apologies that I can’t make this more comfortable for you.” At Koren’s stubbornness, he smiled. “Please, I was about to sit.”

Koren carefully sat, acknowledging the helping hand Jon gave him. “My status has been revoked my Lord, I am no longer ambassador.” He continued before Rufus had the chance to interrupt.

"However I believe you have a problem that I may be able to help you with."

Rufus shrugged, "It's becoming common knowledge, the Cassai army is just over a day away. We can retreat so we don't get mashed up against the walls of your fortress but it means Dulcin may be freed and I want him. He's the key to this whole mess."

"The nobility have sworn fealty?"

"When we reunited them with their families yes, but they're not happy about the situation we're in and I'm not surprised."

"Dulcin has ruled with an iron fist for over fifty years my Lord, and his rule has become stricter and more tyrannical over the last few years. There are few who serve him out of any love or remember any different. They simply need an alternative and you need to give them one."

"We're not in court Koren, call me Rufus." He gave his lightening quick smile and sobered. "Dulcin's willingness to sacrifice the women and children disgusted the family. They were willing to put up with most of his idiosyncrasies but that crossed a line."

"I have been aware of the shortcomings of both our cultures for a long time Rufus. Most I dealt with however there have been certain problems with our own that disgusted me once I became aware of them." The flat statement made Mika wince inside. Her father had to put aside his personal feelings about his own country and government to deal with another's for their benefit.

Rufus allowed his moment of reflection until Koren stirred and said, "Give me a horse and a guard and let me go to where the army is. I presume that Breklyn will be leading them, he is the most likely and if not then I am known by him and the other commanders may listen if he hears what I have to say."

"You're not in a fit state for anything, you can barely stand."

"We do not have time for arguing over this. I will swear my fealty and then represent Ackbarr." Koren's voice was firm, "I am one of the few that can persuade them. If anything, my obvious mistreatment will help."

"What if they think it was us?"

"Breklyn knows I was brought in by Dulcin and that I would not have been let out again. They also saw Dulcin order my son to be murdered."

Mika started in shock, Petron - dead? Aurin hadn't mentioned that, surely he would have done. The image of the skinny child dancing around and playing the fool for his older siblings' attention rose in conflict with the tall man with the look of surly amusement in his eyes. So many things had happened over the last few weeks that she couldn't even begin to grieve for him. He'd been twisted beyond redemption and yet he was still her little brother. She forced herself to pay attention to the pair in front of her.

"Is Elian here?" At Rufus' nod, he said, "Bring him here and ask him his opinion. Elian would be a good choice to accompany me, he is also well known and if he is seen to have changed sides then it will help."

As the tall Cassai was brought over, Koren stood in front of Rufus. "I will swear fealty." He tried to kneel and nearly fell over, Rufus caught him. The whispered conversation made it apparent to all that Rufus wasn't happy about the state Koren was in and that Koren was insisting. Rufus gave in and helped him down to one knee. He spoke the words and Rufus helped him to sit again.

"You will be my spokesperson for the Cassai and that position will continue until either you retire or choose a replacement. Keep the title Ambassador for the moment, we'll think of another later."

Little was private here and Mika could see the soldiers watching and knew everyone would know what had happened between their Commander and the Cassai ambassador. The Cassai watching was introduced as Elian and Koren's plans explained.

"Ambassador Koren is correct." Elian said, "Dulcin is feared. Ackbarr has him penned and Dunbarin has surrendered. It is only a matter of time."

He looked more than a little uncomfortable with his turncoat status. Mika had heard about the reunion of the men with their families and their subsequent anger over what had happened in the tunnels. These men had been brought up to think that they were the elite and to expect everything at their fingertips. Their status as part of the royal family making them arrogant as well as the subconscious cats that slept within them. Mika had seen some of the older children beginning to react to the smoke and noise in the tunnels, under stress at that age it manifested itself for the first time. It was going to take some delicate balancing once all this was over to keep them happy and Mika hoped Rufus and her father would be up to it.

"They are unlikely to know we are here until their scouts arrive. As far as I know they are only aware of Dunbarin under attack."

Elian replied, "The tunnels were flooded before we could get through them Lord Rufus, with you blocking the entrance there is no other way out. Dulcin was raging over the lack of information."

Rufus chewed his thumb, thinking. "You'll need clothes for your status, we'll find something.

Go sleep and eat until we've everything sorted, you'll need your strength."

Koren nodded, not quite a bow which Rufus ignored as he helped him up. Mika rushed over to take his arm and he smiled at her. Elian was escorted back to his comrades who were still being kept in a corner of the camp. While they were in theory allies now, both they and Rufus understood that nothing would be certain until he'd winkled Dulcin out and had control of the army. The smell of cooking wafted from one of the small fires, the smoke filtering through the tree canopy.

Her father sniffed appreciatively, "I could do with some more food." He sounded wistful.

"I'll get you some, come and sit down first."

She left her father in Jon's care and went to find the food. The usual small game stew had been replaced by fish from Dunbarin, more supplies were coming in every day. If her father could talk to the commanders and persuade them to surrender… She sighed at the thought of no more fighting. Most of those in the army would be owners of small holdings and shop keepers, Cassai had never had much of a standing army. The Commanders would be from the elite ranks of the royal family, their orders coming straight from Dulcin – would they stand true to their orders or listen to reason?

Mika brought a bowl back to her father who had been sitting against a tree with his eyes closed.

He opened them as she came up. "Is that a Cassin?" He gestured at Stafa lounging nearby.

Her stomach twisted, "No but one of his parents might have been."

Sensing her discomfort, Koren nodded and began to eat slowly. He paused as Kaylan appeared and walked over to Stafa on his blind side. Stafa rolled over and swiped at him. They tussled with no malice in their fighting, their claws half sheathed. Stafa eventually gave Kaylan a ringing thump across the ear and they sprang apart. Kaylan shook his head and they both began to groom themselves. Kaylan came up and began to lick Stafa's face, nuzzling. Stafa stretched, enjoying it until they sprawled out together.

"Do you think your brother is happy?" Koren had been watching while he ate.

"As much as he can be. I doubt he remembers much about being human anymore."

"I wondered about your mother when I was being held prisoner. It helped, imagining her in the forests. She loved to change, she'd tell me about everything with this look of joy on her face." He trailed off.

Mika was unused to this vulnerability. "Mama always seemed so calm…"

He chuckled, a breathless little sound, strange to hear coming from her father. "She wasn't. Your mother would make herself ill from growing the Vineflowers in her desperation to stop you both changing. The times I found her on her bed, screaming into her pillow and would tell her to go out."

"Go out?"

"To change." Her father looked at her calmly, "I loved to see her as a cat, everything was in balance but she wouldn't leave you children."

"Cassin don't, I've found that out." Mika pressed on, "We have Cassin here, you can speak to them and find out more."

Koren smiled wearily, "I'd like that, having read so much about them." He leaned back, "I've not seen your mother since she left the night we found that Deon had changed. It would be nice to see her."

“She probably won’t recognise us. Jehanne, the leader of the Cassin said that when the final changing’s been delayed so long then the decline tends to happen very quickly. The twins are here though.” His face brightened through his tiredness. “Papa, why did you say Kaylan shamed you? Was it his changing? What happened?” She’d never had the chance to ask this question, the time had never felt right and then Petron had arrived. Mika dropped her head and found herself unable to continue – Petron was dead.

“How could him changing shame us?” The question hung in the air until Mika, flushing, finally managed to look her father in the face. His was soft, “When we left for Ackbarr, all those years ago, I remember how much Kaylan loved travelling through the mountains. He was full of wanting to tell you everything, constantly wishing you were with us so he could share it. He missed you Mika.” Tears began to threaten and she scrubbed at her face.

“We travelled to Fenin on the way to Ackbarr, I had thought it good to give him as much experience as possible of the world outside Cassai. He found a girl he liked, a pretty little thing, she was as fascinated by him as he was by her. Her family offered him the chance to go with them to their country residence. He begged me to let him go. I spoke to them and found them both welcoming and open to their daughter’s wishes. Your mother and I had spoken of wanting to get you both out of Cassai. Neither of us wanted you used.

“I agreed to Kaylan’s pleas and sent one of my trusted aide’s with him although he promised to stay out of mischief. The girl’s father suggested I spoke to Mekhi when I mentioned about you. I spent the time talking to Mekhi, he saw opportunities in your future marriage with his son and I felt that Rylan was young enough to grow with you.

"The family came back the next week without Kaylan, the girl was wild with grief. It was only afterwards that I heard what had happened."

"What?" Mika could barely breathe.

"Kaylan had dealt with all the teasing and rough housing from the local boys with dignity. I had worried with the wild streak in him but he had behaved well until one evening he was set upon by some older youths. They'd heard he wanted to marry the Fenin girl and had objected. They decided to teach him a lesson. They over-powered him, tied him up and took him down to the local gorge."

Koren looked at her soberly, "None of them returned."

"How did you find out about this?"

"There was an inquest with the local elders. Other youths came forward to admit they'd overheard what had been planned, that they'd not meant any harm. They actually had a certain admiration for Kaylan, he'd wanted to find out all about them, to become friends."

She said softly, "He was good at that." Mika remembered the arrogant boy, laughing with the others and yet generous to a fault.

"We visited the gorge and it was plain to me what had happened, Kaylan had changed. Precisely what had triggered it I can't say but there was carnage around…" Koren trailed off and Mika's mind went back to waking in her room next to her dead husband.

Koren took a deep breath, "We tried to find Kaylan but the locals were up in arms about finding the wild animal that had attacked their sons. They didn't care about the one extra body missing. I believe they drove Kaylan further away and he was unable to find his way back. At that point we couldn't stay any longer, we were being viewed with suspicion."

"And yet you still married me to Mekhi."

"Yes and it is something I deeply regret but I had made promises and he held me to them." Koren's fists clenched, "He had powerful friends as a merchant and we were desperate to get you out of Cassai before the truth was discovered about your brother. You would have been incarcerated."

Mika nodded, her head bowed. She swallowed and said, "Then you met Lin and told him about Kaylan."

"I met Belindros as he left Ackbarr, after I had seen you in Fenin. I thought he would be able to look further without arousing suspicion. I still hoped that we'd be able to help Kaylan, although I didn't mention that he'd changed. I knew he'd had suspicions about your mother from some of the questions he'd asked, however I felt some things were too private to tell.

"Belindros found you and thought you were Kaylan. I hadn't mentioned you were in Fenin, I hadn't thought I'd needed to." Her father took a deep breath, "You asked me how Kaylan changing could shame us. It wasn't that, he'd done everything he could and I had been proud of him. Your mother was wild with grief when she heard that he had killed in his other form." He said softly, "She didn't mean it as you took it."

Mika persisted, "And then Jace found him."

"Jace… Jace had changed in the years since I'd known him. By the time I met him in Keira's fathers company, he was no more than a hired killer. If you can imagine him as a youngster much like Kaylan had been then you'd not be far off from his character. Because he knew about your mother, I had to step carefully around him and he knew it. He enjoyed the power over me which the boy I'd known would never have approved of."

"Jehanne let me read a book that had some of his written memories in. Selene, her daughter is actually his too."

"She's your half-sister?"

Mika chuckled, "She's a pain in the backside."

Koren hesitated and said, "Jace came back for you." Mika stared in shock at his admission. "He came back years after he'd left us. I'd married your mother, I'd been working my way into a position of authority, I was determined to shield her the best I could. He found me and wanted to take you all with him."

Her lips were numb, "When… you said no…"

"You are welcome to blame me for this one thing but I refused him to go near you. We argued and he left, after I threatened to tell the family that he'd been here. You must have been about ten or so. He refused to tell me where he'd take you and I'd grown to love all of you."

"And mother?"

"I never told Ayanna. She would have gone with him in an instant."

"She wouldn't have left us."

"She would have taken all of you to be with him." He drew a deep breath, "However I don't believe she would have coped, she never recovered from her solitary upbringing in the compound. As both Jace and I found out when we escaped due to the family finding out about her changing, she struggled outside the small world she'd grown up in."

Those trips out that they'd never been allowed on, her mother had always been snappy for days both before and after. Mika and Kaylan had always assumed it was due to the excitement of going, now she could see it was a terror of being away from familiarity. "And yet you loved her."

"You have no idea of how beautiful your mother was, wild and at one with nature, how could I not love her?" Her father's face was wistful.

"The words Jace left were similar." She ran through what she'd discovered in the book and what Jehanne had told her and Koren nodded and said that what had been written was correct. "Papa, Jace said that Mama used to make up stories, was this true?"

"Yes, she had so little Mik..Mikon." He stumbled over her name, he would have called her Mika in private and she missed it. "We tried to bring in servants with children so you had those of your own age to play with. She had no one."

Looking back on who she'd thought her mother was and finally talking to her father about who she'd actually been was difficult. Layers had been added to the calm woman she thought she'd known and now would never know any better. She was desperate to spend time with her father in a way she'd not been able to and in the knowledge that her own time was limited.

"I have Lin's diaries, he spoke of meeting Mama when you'd been caught and how she stuck to one story all through her questioning."

"She was so brave during that time, remember she had little experience outside the compound. We had agreed on our story before we were caught and I think your mother told it so many times that she finally believed it was the truth. I saw no reason to say otherwise. While it bothered me that Jace had been cast out, I will never regret the time spent with her and being father to you all. I believe that your mother was as happy as she could be as well."

The image that came to Mika's mind was the one as she'd left with her new husband, that of her mother burying her head into her husband's shoulder. The grief in that gesture, her oldest son probably dead and his twin sister leaving to live in a place far away and her turning to the one person who'd stood by her all that time. "What a mess we are."

"True." Koren didn't shy away.

The silence extended between them, the murmurings of the soldiers around them intruding. The final pieces of the puzzle slotted into place, how could she ever have thought her father embarrassed by Kaylan's changing? He'd lived in the compound with them for so many years, the taboo over speaking about it lightened and then lifted. If Rufus could win then she would have choices for once, real choices. The Cassin wouldn't be persecuted, they'd have the chance to live like people, albeit people with an extra dimension to them. She tried to imagine Cassai and Cassin children playing together and failed. There were so many possibilities for the two cultures. Mika turned to her father and asked him that very question.

Koren smiled wearily, "You are forgetting, I did see Cassai and Cassin children playing together. The only difference was that they didn't know it."

She blinked, her childhood years of racing and playing with the servant's children. Mika opened her mouth to speak and noticed her father's eyes closing. "You need to sleep."

He smiled again and let her take his bowl and cover him with a blanket without protest.

Chapter 13

Rufus called Koren over several hours later and they withdrew from the majority of the soldiers to plot tactics. Robes and horses had been found but the new clothes didn't hide how he'd lost weight or the pallor from being shut up for so long. Koren would be leaving with a good force of both Cassai, Ackbarr and Cassin men. Mika had seen the spark in her father's eye at the thought of the negotiations despite him still being exhausted.

Mika left her father and Rufus talking, she'd been formulating an idea of her own, although she wasn't sure what Rufus would think of it. She sat and honed her rapier, wiping it down with an oiled rag while she thought.

Jon sat with her, "You're plotting something."

"Dulcin isn't going to let anyone near him, the Cassin only got out because of the children."

"Rufus has the Cassai to hunt Dulcin down, they've made their decision Mika."

She shook her head, "He's got something else planned, that's why Aurin hasn't come back." She couldn't explain the uneasy feeling she was getting.

"So you're going in alone."

"No, I'll take Stafa." Mika looked down at the cat beside her, "He'll help protect me."

"And what about me? When do I protect you Mika?" His voice had an edge of anger.

She tried not to hear it, "I want you to look after my father. He's weaker than he wants to admit. I want you to go with him when he speaks to the commanders. I need to know he'll be alright."

“I’ll look after her.” The voice came from the trees and they both jumped. Stafa gave a low rumble as Jehanne and Hal walked into the small clearing.

Mika gave Jehanne an assessing look, she was still looking unfocussed as though she were sleep walking. “What’s going to stop you from changing? I can’t deal with both of you going rogue.”

“I want Dulcin removed.” The older woman’s hands clenched. “I can’t hold on much longer, I need this finished.” The large cat nuzzled her thigh and she sprawled down next to him.

“What about him?” Mika nodded at Hal.

The arms tightened, “He’ll do as I say.”

Mika took a deep breath, this wasn’t what she’d wanted but it was better than nothing. “Happy?” she asked, knowing that Jon wasn’t.

“No, but take care. I’ll see Rufus about going with your father.” He got up and walked away without pausing to hug her. He wouldn’t stop her but he didn’t have to show he wasn’t happy.

“Right, we’d better leave now then.” She jerked her head at the two cats and one human and walked in the other direction.

Between her and Jehanne, they had little problem in getting past the Cassin soldiers guarding the entrance to the cat door. Rufus could give all the orders he liked but Jehanne was still their boss and Mika wondered what he thought of it or if he even knew. She found herself on edge again as they walked through the narrow tunnel. There was the remains of the smoke lingering and a dampness underfoot which suggested that the water levels might have risen further.

Jehanne raised her lantern and found the lever, it didn’t want to move. Mika helped her pull it and braced herself against the wall to shove at the door.

Both cats jumped back at the surge of water as it finally opened. Mika swore at her boots getting soaked and froze, waiting to see if it rose any further. It didn't, settling at ankle height into a continuous stream.

It was quiet in the abandoned library, no noise could be heard. Hal stalked in first, his ears flat against his head. Stafa followed, swinging his own head to gain a better idea of his surroundings from his single eye. The smell of old books rose over the smoke and damp, so much knowledge they'd had in here, centuries worth and it was gone. She could only hope they'd stacked the books and scrolls somewhere safe. They crept in, aware of every sound they made echoing in the empty room.

Jehanne spoke into the silence, "We'll need to go down a bit first before we go up to where Dulcin held court." Mika gestured her forwards, the forlorn shelves bothering her more than she liked to admit.

The corridor dipped as Jehanne had promised and the cold waters crept higher. She swore softly as it poured over the edges of her boots. Jehanne appeared in a dream again, swinging her head first one way and then the other, echoing Hal in front and Mika wondered what she was going to do once she'd found Dulcin. The water crept higher to mid-thigh and the cats raised their heads, surging forwards, halfway between swimming and walking. The current tugged at her legs, urging her back.

"Are we going much deeper?"

Jehanne raised a hand to hush her and Mika waited, shivering, her rapier held high to stop it getting wet. If they had to go much deeper, then they wouldn't get through, Dulcin would be trapped in here. The thought of the soft stone collapsing as it wore through wasn't worth thinking of.

"There have been Cassin here. Young ones."

"Ours?"

"No. I don't recognise them."

"How come they are here then?"

"We are all related, remember? There are bound to be changers cropping up."

Mika felt stupid, if she and her brother had happened then yes, others would as well. "Can Hal deal with them?" Stafa hadn't even bothered to challenge the larger cat.

"Maybe." The answer didn't reassure. "They will regard this as their own territory and we are intruders. We need to go this way."

Both cats surged forwards leaving Mika swearing again at the water waving over her upper thighs. The water slowly went down as they climbed and the cats shook themselves, looking disgusted in the dim light. She tipped the water out of her boots and felt the same.

All she could hear was the plop and rush of water, her eardrums ached with the strain of trying to listen beyond it. Mika raised her lantern, took a firm grip of her rapier and wondered what any younger relations would be like and what she could do to protect herself. Those memories she had of Selene changing years ago in the woods near Tatton and when they'd followed the trail to find Lissina, leaping and playing in the dark and she knew she wouldn't be able to hurt them - they were children.

Hal paced to the front, growling briefly at Stafa who showed his teeth but made way for the large cat.

"I think we go further to the right now." Jehanne's voice was soft.

"Think?"

"It's been a long time Mika. I explored when I was an indulged child here." She chuckled, "You are shocked? All of us Cassin were royal family until we showed signs of changing or at least that is what they led us to believe." Her voice darkened, "I remembered coming this way, I must have been about six or so. I was shooed away by the guards with smiles. It didn't work, I found a way when they weren't watching. I'd been looking for a friend, an older lad. Thinking about it, maybe that was why I followed Jace around."

"And?" Mika kept an ear out for noises.

"I found him in a cage in a room with viewing platforms all around it, close to the top of the fortress. I suspect it was some sort of theatre now, only the shows were tests for my kind." Her voice faltered and then strengthened again, "I had come into one of the unoccupied platforms and watched in the dark. There was a brazier with a bunch of herbs on the coals and a man wafting the smoke towards my friend. My friend… I can't remember his name now… he was fighting something inside himself… flinging himself around the tiny cage…trying to get away from the smoke." Jehanne was panting and Mika slid a hand into hers. It was cold.

"It seemed to take ages. They poked him with sticks, slashed at him and did everything they could to force him to the point where eventually he changed. The people watching from the other alcoves applauded and shouted but I knew it wasn't for my friend's achievement. I stayed in the alcove and cried silently while they left. I wanted my friend back, for the animal in the cage to be free. He was beautiful, all big paws and soft spots in his fuzzy coat… I knew there was nothing wrong with him being as he was, it felt right and natural to me but not in that room. Not in that cage…

"Then another man came onto the stage. The look in his eyes, it was like there was a beast inside him that had never shown its face. It was enough to shock me into listening. The first man referred to him as Dulcin and even I knew that this was the person who had power over all the family despite never having seen him. He made a comment about this being a fine beast and that he would use it for his own purposes. I didn't know what he meant, only that I hated him then as I'd never hated anyone in my six years. The cage was taken away and I never saw my friend again."

"I'm sorry." The words felt inadequate.

Jehanne shook herself, "It was a long time ago, the cat overlays so much emotion at my age. It is unusual for it to come through so much." She jerked her head up as Hal snarled. "Beware!"

They'd come into a more open space, the noise of the water echoing around them. The light flickered as she raised the lantern above her head. Hal and Stafa were both looking up, crouching and ready to spring. Mika abruptly realised she was a target as she heard the scrape of a claw across stone and the shadows moved. Both Hal and Stafa launched themselves towards her, Stafa aiming lower to catch her at midriff height and knocking her onto her backside. She desperately tried to keep the lantern above the knee high water and failed.

They plunged into darkness. There were the snarls of Hal and his unknown assailant and Mika could feel the brush of Stafa's wet fur as he stood over her. The snarl of her own cat wanting to take over and plunge her teeth into fur shocked her more than the cold of the water. The growling and thrashing came to a close and Mika held herself still, not knowing what had happened.

"Jehanne?" She could smell blood, the iron taint spreading through the water she sat in. Mika pushed Stafa off and stood hurriedly, not wanting to think about it covering her clothes.

"I'm here. Hold this." A grasping hand found her arm and shoved a small cylinder into her hand. A spark showed Jehanne's face briefly and again as she bent to light the candle Mika was holding. The steady glow showed the tunnel and Hal standing over a submerged form. No chance to heal, the cat's face was underwater. She winced at the blood around his mouth, that would have been a cousin, a younger man or woman brought up here and with little choice over his or her actions.

Jehanne reached down to brush the prone body. "Family," she said, echoing Mika's thoughts. "I'm sorry little one."

Mika felt around with her foot and brushed against the lantern. Fishing it out she found that the glass was broken. It was still useful to carry the candle so she stuck it in and tried not to think about any other changers that they might come across.

The next appeared as they came out of the water, the two cats shaking themselves dry. Jehanne had bent to empty a boot out, while she held the lantern and was taken by surprise. Mika had crouched, ready to use her rapier if needed. The cat almost seemed maddened, ears flat against its head. It took no notice of Hal or Stafa's larger size and attacked without hesitation.

"What I don't understand is why they're all attacking, and singly. They would normally give us a wide berth."

"What do you mean? You said we're on their territory."

"Yes but these are only adolescents, they wouldn't attack Hal or even Stafa under normal circumstances. You've seen your brother deferring. I would have expected an older or larger cat."

"Maybe there aren't any."

"Why? What's happened to them?" Animal. The word echoed around her brain as the next cat attacked. Hal was beginning to slow down, even he couldn't keep fighting off each and every cat.

"Damn." Jehanne was holding her repeater bow and trying to aim it. She dropped her aim as Stafa grabbed hold of the other cat's spine and shook it. "I can't get a clear shot with them fighting like that."

A smell drifted across them, and Mika breathed deeply without realising it. "When I was caught, I got the feeling they didn't tolerate changers." The twist of the man's face as he brought the smoking herbs towards her. She shook her head, trying not to remember. The lives she'd saved as a Medici, she wasn't an animal, it must have counted for something. The same twist in her half-brother's face. It hadn't mattered that they'd had the same mother, the same upbringing and in the same household.

"There would have been others. The family is bred too close for there not to be." Jehanne looked tense in the half light. Mika tried not to look at the body the two cats had dropped. The soft fur and too large paws proclaimed it young. "Something happened to them. What have they done?"

"I was nearly given to someone called Phineas."

"Phineas?" Jehanne jumped, startled. She called out to Hal, "Don't move so fast." Both cats ignored her, sniffing at the air and loping forwards. "I remember a Phineas. He was my age."

The thought made Mika stop briefly, she'd not realised that Jehanne would have contemporaries alive in Dubari and realised that if Phineas wasn't a changer then he'd have no problems staying human. She nearly snorted, recalling the cold eyes boring into hers and the voice asking for her. Human wasn't quite what she'd call what he was.

They hurried after the two cats. They were swiping at each other, in as foul a mood as Mika felt. She found herself brooding as they walked, the injustice of her situation biting. She was useless, the two cats taking on all the fighting before she could help and even then she wasn't sure she could kill. Why was she even trying, Dulcin could drown in his cold grave, no one would care, the only thing that was keeping her going was the fact that Rufus needed Dulcin alive. Jehanne was muttering to herself as well, throwing the occasional hard look her way. Hal had disappeared into the dark beyond the candlelight, Stafa close at his heels.

"Stafa." Mika called to him, intending to walk away and tell Rufus to leave Dulcin to drown or have the place collapse on him. Stafa stopped to look at her in the light. The snarl of her inner cat woke her out of her brooding just as a clang reverberated through the tunnel. Stafa jumped towards them, his fangs bared.

"Hal!"

Jehanne ran towards the noise and Mika's fingers caught air. She fought her unreasonable mood to chase after Jehanne - they had to stay together.

"Jehanne…"

The candlelight bounced off black strips in front, turning into metal bars between them and Hal. Jehanne moaned and grabbed hold of them, trying to rock them loose. They shifted a little and Hal snarled, showing his teeth. There was a pressure plate under Hal's feet where he'd sprung the trap, the light showed little else apart from a mist in front of his face.

"Wait," Mika took hold of the other woman, waving the candle to try and see more.

"No, I can't. I must get him out." Jehanne appeared to be sinking into a dream, her eyes wide. Mika stared, shaking off the funk she was in. Jehanne's pupils looked strange in the candle light, far larger than they should be. She swung the lantern over to Hal and he startled, his eyes were the same, his ears flat and muscles tense. Finally she caught a stronger whisp and followed it to a small container and as if seeing it made a difference, she smelt something waft in her direction.

"No Jehanne, listen to me. There's something wrong here." Ignoring her, Jehanne swung her arm around and knocked the lantern out of Mika's hand. It went flying towards the wall and Mika dove for it. She saw the fleeting shadow of Jehanne running the other way before the candle went out.

In the darkness, Mika could feel Hal movements behind the bars, he was pacing, agitated. A snort and a chirrup came from her other side and the sound of Stafa shaking his head. Hal roared a challenge, the noise reverberating and making her ears ring. The bars shook as Hal threw himself at them, a terrifying sound in the dark.

The breeze of air as one of his paws swiped close by, she cringed against the wall and went colder. The wall was damp underneath her hand. The walls had been cool when she'd been down here before but never wet, was the water coming through this high up? Mika pulled herself to her feet, she had to get out of here. Hal was trapped and there was no way she was going to even attempt to free him in this mood…

Mika stopped as Stafa growled. Hal was still flinging himself at the bars, going frantic as he tried to get at her. She raised her head and sniffed, there was a tang to the air, she'd thought it was just the smell of water filled caves but no, there was something else.

Her irritation twisted, was this some herb she didn't know about? It wasn't the one they'd used when she'd been caught and she knew about the ones the Cassai used to discourage Cassin by burning it on small fires on the easy routes out of the mountains but this was different again. She swore, there was so much she didn't know, so much that could be used against her.

There was quiet, Hal had stopped his frenzy. She could feel how he was listening and tensed herself. A faint sound came from further up the tunnel. Hal growled and she heard the thud of his large feet as he sprang away.

Stafa leant against her, shoving gently. "Okay, I'm getting up," she grumbled.

What to do now? Jehanne had the dry matches, hers were wet through. The thought of wading through pitch black tunnels full of water didn't appeal and the idea of the rock above her head collapsing was equally unappealing. She sighed and shoved down her irritation, manufactured or real, she'd have to either find Jehanne or a way out further up.

She ran her fingers through Stafa's damp fur, feeling the dry undercoat. If the smell was affecting Hal, making both her and Jehanne irritable then what would it do if she changed? Stafa appeared unaffected. She poked her inner cat and sighed, it was curled up tightly. It didn't like it here and she didn't blame it.

"Can you find Jehanne, Stafa?" Her voice sounded odd in the quiet. He nuzzled her thigh and stepped away. Mika grabbed a fistful of his ruff and hoped they didn't come across any more changers – she'd be a sitting duck in the dark.

Chapter 14

Mika walked, one hand on Stafa's ruff, the other holding her unsheathed rapier. Stafa would periodically drop his nose to the floor and she would bend with him, not wanting to let go. She couldn't tell if the smell was less intense or if she was becoming used to it. Her irritation was replaced by worry, all the ventilation shafts were blocked and the only way out was to access one of the small windows on the front of the cliff or through the cat tunnel. Having spent days staring up at those windows, she knew they'd probably be too small for her to wriggle through, let alone Stafa.

Tears trickled down her face, this place was supposed to be the bastion of her country, all the knowledge seated here and the mainstay of the elite. It was being destroyed and she'd had a part in it. What she'd thought her country was, what her people were, had been a lie. She felt fifteen again, betrayed by those she'd thought were supposed to look after her. How could Ackbarr deal with this? She paced, thinking of Selene and Tamar and his fierce protectiveness of his new found daughter. Could they prove that Ackbarr and Cassai could live together?

Mika shook her head, she'd proved that already with the smiles and waves she had when walking through the city, the acceptance of those needing her help. She was seen as Medici first, not Cassai, Enos' words had been correct. Once the ports and the new highway through the mountains were open to all, traders would come and people of many different colours and ideas. Change in the isolated country would be slow, but it would happen. She pictured Tahiri playing with other children, other changers and raised her chin. Tahiri would never be told to leave her family. All she had to do was find Dulcin and get him back to Rufus.

Stafa stopped and made a short noise, he wasn't sure where to go. Mika could feel his pelt moving as he swung his head. A noise came from one direction and she tilted her own, "Let's go that way."

Mika wasn't sure what the noise was, only that it might lead to some way of getting light. As they walked, her misgivings grew. The smell became stronger again and as the noises became louder, she recognised them as snarling. Cats were fighting ahead, the screeching and yowling made the fur stand up on the back of Stafa's neck and she felt herself trying to do the same. Her own cat was curling up tighter and she welcomed it as she gritted her teeth against the strange smell.

A long drawn out screech was cut off and she heard a rattling of bars. Mika tried not to imagine the teeth crunching through a spine or back legs raking through belly fur. Her steps quickened, waving her rapier in front of her in an effort not to bump into anything. She winced as it struck stone, knowing it would blunt quickly.

The roar sounded closer, she was sure it sounded like Hal. The large chest gave a deeper note compared to the less developed youngsters - what was going one there? Stafa was rumbling under her hand. She stopped to crouch down and grabbed his head, trying not to think about the huge jaws under her hands.

"Don't even think about it. I'm not losing you."

To her surprise, he butted at her chest and knocked her back onto the floor. There was an element of possessiveness in the tongue that scraped her cheek and the thought of kitten pushed through.

“Ow.” Mika stood, rubbing her backside. “I forgot, you’re a randy furball that’s not going to let me get away. I suppose it had to be useful sometime.” He waited for her to grab his ruff again and they walked towards the sound.

The light appeared suddenly as they rounded a corner. Mika stood blinking and trying to see through her streaming eyes. The noise was very close now, it seemed to be coming from below them. She slowed, waiting for her eyes to adjust.

The tunnel opened out a little, stopping into one of the many viewing platforms normal in Dubari. The light and noise was coming from below, Mika crept up, knowing she’d not be seen in the dark above.

Many other platforms opened out onto this room. She went cold as she made sense of the scene, cages were stacked around the edges of the room, half of them empty. The other half were full of pacing cats, ears back and spitting. Two braziers smoked gently, a pile of herbs on each of them. A tunnel of bars led from fronts of the cages to a larger cage where…

Mika nearly threw up as the ball of fur and claws rolled into view. It was Hal desperately fighting another cat. Gouges ran down the large body, blood staining the grey fur. Other dead cats came into focus, bellies ripped out, heads at awkward angles. Some had changed partially, a hand covered in fur, a face distorted by teeth as they’d tried to heal.

A final crunch and Hal staggered to his feet, shaking the smaller cat hanging limply from his mouth and Mika mourned the waste of life. A clang and a cage door opened. Another cat flowed down the tunnel and she saw the man, watching with a smile on his face. He'd not changed much in over ten years, he'd just become thinner, his face harder.

Phineas turned to a side entrance, "He is a strong beast my lord." A shadow shifted, a leg being crossed. An inaudible comment was made and Phineas bowed. "Would you wager this will be the last?"

Mika stared, who was the person in the shadows? A growl distracted her, the fresh cat had reached the entrance of the cage and sprung. Hal's weariness was evident, no cat could deal with constant attacks or with that amount of blood loss. He couldn't change anymore, he was too far gone. Mika steadied herself, she needed to get down there. It was a fifteen foot drop, ten if you jumped onto the cage. She didn't fancy doing that if Hal was still in there but she needed to douse those herbs, the irritation was bubbling underneath everything, it made it hard to think.

"No." The scream was almost feline, a yowl that echoed through the chamber. Phineas jerked his head up and out of the corner of her eye she saw the leg move back in the shadows. A black streak shot through the air and punched Phineas in the chest. He folded like a collapsed tent, his face twisting in shock. Other shots followed and Mika forgot everything as Jehanne launched herself off another platform, her eyes wild.

That other man, she didn't think Jehanne had seen him, she had to get down to help Jehanne. She'd dropped the crossbow at the same time as she'd had jumped and it had been left where it had fallen.

"Get the braziers Jehanne."

The tall woman ignored Mika's shout, she was punching Phineas. He was unable to hold her back, doubled up around the bolt. The sound of fists hitting human flesh, how Jehanne was staying human she didn't know. Stafa backed up and jumped, whistling past her and she swore. Mika sheathed her rapier and gripped the edge of the platform, hoping that the other man didn't have a crossbow and that Hal was distracted with the other cat. She dropped onto the bars of the cage where Hal was fighting and scrambled over the edge.

Jehanne was still hitting the larger man and he was a mess. His face was blue and choking. Mika knew there was poison on that bolt, it was just a matter of time. She tipped the braziers over, stamped on the ashes, picking out the herbs and flung them to one side.

Jehanne had stopped, exhausted. Her face was tragic, gazing at the cage with her mate in it. "Hal."

Mika had to stop this, one last death and it didn't matter what she felt about killing innocent victims. She picked up the crossbow and sighted along it, waiting for her chance and breathing through her concentration. Jehanne flung herself at the cage, in the way and Mika pulled her to one side and knelt, her finger tightening.

Hal spasmed as the other cat got a firmer grip and they froze for a moment, Hal's struggles getting weaker. Mika flicked the trigger and the bolt lodged into the other cat. Jehanne was standing, her hands against the bars, tears running down her face. "Do something."

"I have, I can't do anything else." Jehanne had used the rest of the bolts firing at Phineas. Mika put the weapon down and tried to hold her, "We need to wait."

"Fuck that." Jehanne pulled away and began fumbling at the entrance to the cage, her fingers stiff. Hal was still struggling, although a lot less. Mika couldn't believe he was still fighting. She squinted, was the other cat slowing? Without warning it suddenly fell sideways, its tongue sticking out. Hal dropped his large head, exhausted.

Jehanne had pulled the cage door open and ran to him. She cradled his head, ignoring the weak growl he gave. "Help him."

Mika slid into the cage, wary of both Hal and the fact that there was that other man around. She could only hope Stafa would watch out for them. The last thing she wanted was to be trapped in here as well. Up close Hal's injuries were immense, blood was pouring out of puncture wounds in his neck. His forearm was crippled and it looked like a back leg had been hamstrung.

"I can't…" She had no medicines here, nothing to help but even she couldn't repair a cut hamstring - he'd be crippled and Hal was no caged cat, used to being fed. He would die in the wild, unable to hunt. "Jehanne, unless he can change to heal himself he'll be useless." She felt the tears begin to stream down her own face.

"No…" Jehanne's fingers ran themselves through the blood soaked ruff, her tears falling onto his face. Hal's rumble became a rusty purr, the loss of blood confusing him as he tried to comfort his mate who was crying over his wounds. Mika could see the dilation of his eyes, it wouldn't be long now. Slowly the wounds ceased to weep and his purr faded. Jehanne struggled to keep his head up and shook him, desperate for a reaction. All she got was a tremor and he lay still in her arms.

Her weeping became louder, starting afresh. Mika stood, having seen death before and knowing Jehanne had to let her sorrow out before she could begin healing. The memory of how she'd held back her grief from Lin's death rose but this was different. Jehanne had expected to start a new life with Hal as a cat, now she had no one. Mika looked at Stafa, sat at the cage door and wondered how she would cope without him? She didn't want her brother when she changed, the one she needed was Stafa.

Mika rubbed her face, they had to be practical, she had a suspicion who that man in the shadows was but she needed to make sure. She looked around, with the herbs and ashes off the braziers, the cats had settled down a little, although they still hissed as she moved. With a guilty look at her friend grieving over her mate, Mika walked out of the cage to inspect Phineas. Mika felt a vicious pleasure as she saw his face had turned black from the poison and Jehanne's beating. A single door led from the room and she pushed it open cautiously.

It was a library and laboratory in one, books and glass bottles competed for space. There were rooms in the Medici building that echoed this place although the Medici ones were for preserving life rather than the study of its death. She picked up a book and flicked through it absently. Diagrams, both of cats and humans dominated and with notes written in a neat hand in the margins. Feeling sick, she shut it quickly. Looking closer in the glass bottles, she found dissected parts, some half way through the change.

Mika came out of the room feeling unclean and realised she'd had a close escape all those years ago. A different note in the sobbing caught her ear. Jehanne was still bent over the big cat, although she was silent now. Stafa moved over to one of the cages and was peering in. He chirruped as she came over.

A girl was curled up in the back and she flinched as Mika came close. The two cats in the cages on either side swiped out, attempting to claw her over to them. There was only a tiny area she had to stay safe in and Mika wondered if it had been deliberate as all the cages were the same size.

Mika crouched down and tried speaking in Cassai, "Are you okay?" The girl flinched further, huddling into herself. She was barely out of childhood, her skinny arms and legs wrapped around herself. "You don't need to worry, I won't hurt you."

The girl refused to answer and Mika suppressed a swear word, she didn't have time to look after children, she had to find out where the man had gone. Jehanne looked fit to stay over Hal's body until the caves collapsed and yet she knew there was one thing that would move her.

She walked over and put a hand on Jehanne's shoulder. "Jehanne, I'm sorry but we need to move."

"Leave me…"

"Jehanne, there are youngsters here, they need you." It was a nasty thing to do and yet there were fifteen changers here who'd never known the reality of their kin or that it was natural and good to do what they did. They'd never stalked through the forest, delighting in their nature. "They are family Jehanne."

Another cry from one of the cages, this time a boy only a little older than the girl. Jehanne's head swung up.

Mika persisted, "I need you to help them Jehanne."

Jehanne's eyes were dead and yet she stood, carefully laying Hal onto the ground. "What are you doing." Her voice was flat.

"I need to go further in. Wait until they've changed and find a way out. Leave the ones who don't, Stafa will deal with them when we come back." She thought for a moment Jehanne's face would crack – Hal could have dealt with all of them if they'd not been under the herb's influence. She watched Jehanne walk up to the cage with the girl inside and start making soft reassuring noises. Mika nodded to Stafa and they left.

Chapter 15

Mika pulled a stool out from Phineas' laboratory and hoped Jehanne wouldn't go in there. She glanced quickly over her shoulder, Jehanne had coaxed the girl out and was talking to another child through the bars of his cage. She smiled sadly, she'd get them out.

She stood on the stool to climb onto the platform where the man had been. Stafa jumped in one easy movement and flicked his tail as they set off down the passageway. They passed the chair, pushed back against the wall.

Mika stopped Stafa and pulled his head to the chair, "Can you follow him?" The large cat flicked his ears back, his face twisting further. "Please Stafa." He stalked off and Mika hoped he was doing as she'd asked.

There were lit wall sconces at intervals, she didn't need the borrowed lantern. Mika decided to put it down close to a light, she could always pick it up on her way back. The lights showed new dark stains on the honey coloured walls. She shivered, how close was the system to collapsing? What damage had the engineers done to the drainage that stopped the soft rock from being worn away? The rain had been horrific in the mountains, they'd seen it coming down while mostly missing the showers.

The corridor became grander, traceries of patterns in the stonework, worn by time and hands. The wall sconces holding the clean smelling oil were carved and had glass fitted to diffuse the light. Mika followed Stafa, watching every doorway, not knowing if anyone else was around and yet knowing the place was abandoned. The corridor ended in a large wooden door. Stafa stopped and raised a paw to scratch, looking at her. She swallowed and drew her rapier.

Mika pushed at the door and Stafa slid in before she could go through. He growled and not needing the warning, she was looking everywhere to look for danger. It was a large room, with carved pillars holding up the roof, and old, rich tapestries showing forest scenes in the Cassai style. She recognised the knotwork on the vineflowers embroidered into the fabric as similar to those her mother used to make. Her heart wept thinking of her mother struggling to weave them together to help keep them safe while feeling physically sick from the smell.

Everything in the room pulled her eyes towards the centre and the steps leading up to the seat at the back. Her gaze was stopped by the man kneeling awkwardly in front, his arms stretched out in supplication and his hands tied to an iron ring pegged into the floor. His back was a mess, shivers ran over his skin and blood showed through the tatters of his clothing. Some of the wounds looked infected, deep red lines running from them and the smell of pus. He was quiet, panting softly, she guessed from shock, he wouldn't last long without treatment and even then...

She almost flung down her rapier to check on him, her Medici training so inbuilt that she nearly forgot where she was. Stafa gave another warning growl and she looked at the chair on the steps. Two cats were wrapped around the chair, so realistically carved that she could tell the larger of the two was male. A man sat there, ramrod straight and so still he might have been one of the carvings. He was old, his hair white and face hard. Lines had settled showing a stubborn personality and narrowed eyes. He looked like her biological father despite his age. She knew who he was, she recognised him from all those years ago when he'd pronounced his judgement on her. This was the man who had imprisoned her mother, threatened both her father and stepfather and tortured many others for the years he'd ruled her country with an iron fist.

"Dulcin." Her voice was flat.

There was no humanity in his face as he studied her, the silence extending between them. Eventually he said, "So, which bloodline did you spring from? You're too old for one from here and too refined for the mountains." He rested his chin on his elbow, "The only one you could be would be Ayanna's offspring, Mika wasn't it." It wasn't a question, he knew precisely who she was. "You would have been her successor, it's a pity you are defective. I'd like to say it's nice to meet you again after so long however I would be lying." His eyes dropped to Stafa, "And that is an animal, not a Cassin. You must be close to changing forever, I can tell you know. Do you intend to mate with it?"

He was provoking her, she deliberately refused to take the bait. Dulcin's hand dropped to caress one of the cats wrapped around the throne. The head and shoulders looked bald and she realised with horror that they weren't stone, they were real. Someone had stuffed dead cats and wrapped them around his chair. Mika took a step closer, seeing the glass eyes winking in the light and felt sick.

He saw her gaze, "You like my companions? This is Uma and her mate, Floran."

"Your daughter…"

The whisper came from the man close to her feet. He had lifted his head an inch to speak and then dropped it down again, this time sideways onto the floor. Mika froze, she knew that voice, had heard it in playful teasing in the dark. Why hadn't she recognised him? The hair was the white blonde he'd bleached it to under the blood clots.

"Yes Aurin, she was my daughter. She betrayed me." A deep anger began to burn in the old man's eyes. "Just like you did. I believe you met Aurin several times Mika, he was a useful spy. Unfortunately a spy is only worth his loyalty and he betrayed that." He caught her look, "Oh yes, he's told me everything."

Mika looked in horror at Aurin's back and the rest of the wounds as he knelt on the stone floor. Stafa's growl jerked her head up as Dulcin stood.

"Why?"

"He was a spy. He chose to betray his country and when I have finished with him he will die painfully in the dark for his crimes."

"Mika, get out of here." Aurin's whispered words broke her heart.

"Listen to him Mika," Dulcin's mimic cauterised the hurt. "He told me everything that happened between you, including the nights you cried in his arms." His face was delighted and he lingered on the words, looking for her reaction.

Mika controlled her shock - she'd never cried a man's arms apart from with Lin. It had frustrated Jon despite him knowing she had problems trusting. Aurin must have lied to Dulcin and flavoured his lies with enough truth to make them believable to this hellish old man. She had to free him somehow, he didn't deserve to die in the dark, no one had ever deserved to die by Dulcin's command. Mika bowed her head, allowing her lids to drop as though fighting tears. Stafa began to creep to the side, reading her minute body language that she was ready to fight.

"He's an arsehole, I never trusted him. What I want to know is, what did you do to my brother? He never did anything to you." She let desperation flavour her voice as she took a step towards Aurin, hoping to distract Dulcin.

"You mean Petron? Ah yes, he was an interesting case. So easy to twist that young man. Jealousy is an easy handle to use."

"You'd know that. You were jealous of the Cassin you couldn't be." She flung the words at him.

Dulcin paused in reaching for the rope around the male cat's neck. "I was destined to rule and I have. I will die ruling."

Mika took another step until she was level with Aurin, studying his hands tied to the ring from under her lashes. Stafa was still creeping through the pillars to the side, she'd have to get him to back Dulcin into a corner and hold him there while she concentrated on cutting Aurin free. She swore at leaving Jehanne behind despite knowing she'd have had problems getting her to think straight with the man responsible for so many problems in front of her. She took a step in front of him and slid her knife out from under her belt, holding it behind her back with her free hand. A childish ruse but she had no other.

"I'm taking you to Rufus and you will die in public to prove you have no power anymore. Cassai and Cassin are going to be living with Ackbarr peacefully together. They've won Dulcin and I'm glad. No Cassin should be ashamed of what they are. I've lived in Ackbarr for years, they've accepted me in a way I've never been accepted here."

His knotted fingers picked up the coiled rope. "You are an animal."

"I'm not the animal in this room." It felt exhilarating to say it aloud.

"Stay back." He flicked the rope and it became a whip. It snapped at Stafa, making him spring back. Mika swore to herself, this changed everything, there was no way she could free Aurin even if he could help himself. Dulcin was still talking, "It's a pity that the herbs don't work on normal cats or even the monsters that arise from the debauched matings. If they had then your pet would have killed you while you stared."

"All those innocent children you have caged for your entertainment." She shuffled closer, trying to distract him.

"Animals, all of them."

"They are your family."

He laughed at her, "I am alpha, I command the family."

"You command nothing Dulcin. All the family have left you, they've sworn themselves to Ackbarr." Her stomach twisted, that is if her father had persuaded the army to switch sides. If they stayed loyal then they'd grind Rufus up against the walls of the fortress he'd emptied.

Stafa lunged and Dulcin retaliated by flicking the whip towards his blind side. Mika dropped her knife next to Aurin and hoped he would be able to cut himself free. She shifted to the side to give Dulcin two targets as Aurin raised his head to stare at the knife, a hopeless look on his face.

"They are nothing." Spit came out of Dulcin's mouth as he spoke, his eyes burning. Despite his obvious madness, Mika felt his commanding presence - he would have had a similar appeal to Rufus when he was younger. She felt sick realising that her brother had had the same and that Jace had shown flashes of it while not in his drug induced nightmare. The brilliance it had originally taken to defeat Ackbarr. Not now, the flexibility had turned to stone, the virtuosity into insanity.

The whip lashed out while she was distracted and her inner cat jumped her back without her being aware. The end coiled around the blade of her rapier, jerked and slid off. She firmed her lips, if that had caught the hilt of her sword then he'd have taken it right out of her hand. She lowered herself into a more defensive position.

"Did you get your pet from the menagerie at Ackbarr Mika?" She stayed silent, not wanting to give him an opening and ignored how his voice caressed her name. She studied his face and the way he held his body, Stafa doing the same on the other side. "I sent an animal changer there years ago, I flicked his eye out when he attacked me and scarred his face. No one else could catch him until I did. He wanted a female and it looks as though he's finally got a willing one. How long have you got Mika?"

Dulcin handled the whip with ease, keeping them at a distance. Sweat was gleaming down his face in the light, he couldn't get away but neither could they get near him. She began to despair, they could do nothing apart from jump out of his way. Stafa had several marks in his thick fur from the barbed end, one was bleeding. His single eye made it difficult for him to pace around and attack from a different angle. Mika was wary of her own face, not wanting to lose an eye as well.

"I'm going to take you back to Rufus for justice. You will die so Cassai and Cassin can have peace."

"Cobwebs and fairy tales. The Cassin were born to rule, it's in our blood. The bleached white Cassai have had that bred out of them…"

He looked ready to go into a rant. Mika interrupted him, "You're not a changer, how would you know? If you were brought up in the Cassin community then you would have been thrown out." A moment's inspiration, "You're the defective."

Dulcin's eyes bulged, "I am Alpha. I rule here and people live and die by my wishes…"

Mika cut in, "See, you're not a cat. They don't care once the pecking order's established. The cats care about family." She lowered her voice, "And you've more than proved you don't."

She jumped out of the way as the whip flicked towards her. "You're presiding over a crumbling ruin Dulcin. The family has sworn itself to Rufus. He understands what they need more than you. The youngsters have been uncaged and Phineas is dead. You have nothing."

To her surprise, Dulcin laughed, "Do you think Phineas was important? I let him play because he was amusing. Young minds are so easy to twist, like plants. Snip one shoot off and they grow in a different direction. Jealousy provides a rich compost you know, all sorts of interesting concepts there to suggest. Your little brother for instance…"

Petron, what lies had this old man whispered into his ear? The jealousies of childhood, they'd all been loved in different ways. The young man who'd come to Ackbarr with the cold amused eyes, who might he had grown into if he'd had the chance? She had to distract Dulcin somehow, make him think she was the easier one to subdue. She was beginning to panic, why hadn't she told Rufus her plans? He'd have sent a contingent of soldiers with her, they'd have dealt with the youngsters and come here. They could have surrounded Dulcin and made him surrender easily, she was arrogant to think she could have captured Dulcin.

She had to deal with this, he was arrogant enough to think she was a weak woman and she only had her inner cat to help and it was curled up tight and sulking after the herbs. Mika let the tip of her rapier droop and his whip snapped out to catch it immediately. Even knowing he'd take that advantage she'd given, she still jumped and he laughed. No rapier, no knife. She daren't look behind her at Aurin, Dulcin would take full advantage.

"Now these odds are more to my liking. Can you still change Mika or have those drugs completely stunted your ability?" He smirked at her expression, "Yes, I heard about your attempts to bury part of yourself. You can't."

She poked her inner cat and it curled up tighter. "How would you know?" Mika spread her hands out, trying to distract him. They had no chance of disarming him, not unless she let him catch her so Stafa could creep up. She swallowed, she didn't want those hands on her.

"My first wife was a full changer. She hated the thought of declining so she tried everything and found she couldn't suppress the cat. I strangled her in the end, she was becoming embarrassing."

"And you killed your daughter for what reason?"

"She committed treason, she and Floran attempted to depose me. I chose to remind everyone the consequences of that by having them here." His voice sharpened, "Less of this talking while you creep around me." The whip snapped out at Stafa as he sprang, wrapping itself around his neck. Stafa checked himself mid-jump at the noose and immediately backed away, shaking his head.

"Animals, they all do the same." Dulcin braced himself against Stafa's pull. The whip tightened and the big cat wheezed, rolling his eye. "Come here Mika."

He held his other hand out, his teeth bared in a grin. Her eyes were fixed on Stafa, his ribs heaving as he tried to breathe and found her own hand reaching out. Dulcin wouldn't be expecting her to fight, if the price of subduing Dulcin was Stafa's life, could she do it? Her own cat wouldn't budge, she couldn't persuade it, Dulcin was alpha and she was on his territory despite his inability to change.

Stafa was sinking to the floor and tears rolled down her face. "Let him go." Her voice cracked.

"A quick death, nothing to cry about. More than that animal deserves." His hand closed around her wrist and pulled her into him. She attempted to struggle and froze at the touch of his dry skin, the memory of Jace looming above her. "It won't take long."

Mika could feel the tension in his body as he fought the cat and marvelled that he'd stopped Stafa so easily. She could feel her breath coming faster - she couldn't move. Gavin was laughing and showing her what to do if she was stupid enough to let go of her weapon. She wasn't strong enough to overpower a man but she might surprise them if she did this or that. Varian's dry voice and penetrating eyes telling her she was a second class Medici if she hesitated, none of it meant anything, the words rambling through her head as she watched the animal she'd hoped to live with, die.

Chapter 16

Mika was mesmerised, unable to move while she watched Stafa slowly being strangled until Dulcin's body jerked and his grip loosened. The cat, up to this point as frozen as she'd been, roared through her body and took it over without bothering to change. She twisted and slammed a hand under Dulcin's chin, pushing him backwards and tucked a foot behind his feet. Dulcin fell hard against the stone floor, his head cracking. He bounced once and she had to stop herself from stamping on his stomach before he lost consciousness.

"Stafa..." It was almost a growl. Mika dragged herself back from the cat and it relinquished control, satisfied with its conquest of the male who'd dominated them. She ran to the big cat, tugging at the whip to pull it away from his throat. He wheezed the air into his lungs, the tip of his tongue poking out and his eye glazing. Mika dragged Stafa's head into her lap. "Don't you bloody die on me."

She massaged his throat, wincing at the long wound from the tightened whip weeping blood. Every breath was a victory, nothing else mattered. It felt like an age before Stafa blinked at the tears falling into his fur. The tongue went in and then lipped at her gently and a rusty purr started. Exhausted, she rubbed his ears, curling herself around the large head in relief.

"Well, what does a man have to do around here to get attention?" The words were weary but still amused. Embarrassed, Mika turned to see Aurin slumped on the floor.

"Aurin, I'm sorry." She put Stafa down and began checking him over, her touch professional.

"You're burning up, I need to get you out of here." That was an understatement, his wounds were infected, she'd rarely seen worse other than those from the poor quarter who were unable to stop work to get help. She pushed the knowledge from her mind that those people rarely recovered.

He shivered, "I'm cold. Mika, you need to get Dulcin out. Tie him up and drag him out of here if you have to. Don't worry about me."

"Shut up. We're all getting out." Mika wrapped the thinner end of the whip around Dulcin's wrists, tugging it tight and checked him over. There was a lump on the back of his skull but the skin hadn't been broken. Her inspection paused as she found her knife buried in his shoulder. "You threw my knife."

"Proud of me?" Aurin was looking paler in the lamp light. Proud wasn't the word, somehow he'd managed to gather enough strength to cut the ropes and throw that knife. The fact that he'd actually hit Dulcin was incredible. She nodded, trying not to show her emotions and knew she was failing.

"Stafa, come here." The big cat pulled himself up and walked over. Mika gave him the whip handle. "I need you to pull on this, we need to bring him with us." Stafa sniffed at the unconscious man and growled. She grabbed the thick fur around his neck and stared into his eye, "Do as I say." Slowly he lowered his head and mouthed the whip.

Mika turned to Aurin, "Right, I'm taking you."

"Leave me…"

She ignored him and pulled him upright. "Don't go all weak on me, keep talking. Come on Stafa." Aurin was a dead weight, his legs refusing to support him. Mika staggered, and partly dragged him towards the door. Stafa picked up the whip and spat it out again. He took one of Dulcin's wrists in his mouth and hauled him across the floor like downed prey. She snorted and decided that he'd survive the experience. Aurin was a different matter, he was shivering and she had to keep him conscious. "Come on, what happened?"

"I was an idiot. He had the youngsters patrolling and they cornered me." His head dropped and then he started again a little louder. "He'd realised I'd betrayed him and was furious, it was worse when he heard the family had sworn themselves to Rufus. I'm going to die Mika."

"We'll see." She grimly refused to think about it.

"Phineas rubbed something onto my back before Dulcin started whipping me… he'd decided putting me into a cage with a youngster would be too merciful. It's going to rot me from the inside out once it's in my bloodstream. Leave me here Mika."

Aurin stumbled and Mika nearly fell with him. "I'm getting you out Aurin." He mumbled something, no longer quite conscious.

There was a rumble from deep underground and a breath of dank air puffed through the still tunnels making the lamps flicker. Mika was tired and they'd not even got back to the laboratory yet. She could see the hair standing up on the back of Stafa's neck and felt her own cat scrabbling at her to get out of this place.

She staggered after the big cat dragging the man, focussing on one step at a time and counting off the number of steps it would take to get to each lamp. Every minute upright and moving was to be celebrated and finally the corridor opened out into the caged area. Stafa dropped Dulcin's wrists and jumped, leaving him in the opening. Mika was nearly flattened by Aurin as she pulled him down. She looked back hopelessly at the larger figure and wondered how to get him down. She left Aurin sat against the wall, he was barely conscious, his skin flushing and going pale.

Stafa was sat at one of the cages. A paw was slashing at him, a continuous low growl coming from it. Mika moved closer and saw a slender male, it must have been younger than her sons with the spots clearly showing on its fluffy coat.

"He won't change cat, leave him be and stop teasing him." The voice was weary until the owner saw Mika. A pair of knuckles appeared, "Can you get me out? The keys are on the table."

"Yes if you can help me. Why didn't you go with the rest?"

"I woke up and the cages around me were empty apart from his." The young man's voice was bitter as he climbed out of the cage. He stretched, "That one hasn't changed since he was tested, some of them don't. I think it's a safety thing."

"We can't leave him, does he have a name?"

"He's just the small one. He spits at everything." Stafa pawed at the cage, ignoring the snarling.

Mika asked, "You can deal with him?" Stafa flicked his ears in distain, he was nearly twice the size of the smaller cat. "Okay, here goes." Mika undid the lock and stepped out of the way and Stafa moved back to allow the cage door to swing open.

The young man laughed as the smaller cat backed away into the shadows of his cage. "All spit, snarl and no bite. Your cat'll have to go and get him out."

Stafa snuffed at the door, looked at her once and then walked in. Considering he'd been caged for so much of his life, he trusted her not to slam the door on them both. There was a brief scuffle with

Stafa pinning the youngster onto his back and staring him out. The smaller cat squeaked its submission and stopped fighting. When Stafa backed out, it stayed there. With an almost human sigh of irritation, Stafa went back in and dragged it out by its neck.

It was a lot smaller than Mika had realised. It snarled at her as she came near and Stafa clouted it. He slapped it down with a heavy paw and began licking its ears roughly.

"That's cute." The young man laughed, "Now you said you needed my help. Shall I carry him?" He indicated Aurin's prone figure.

Mika went through the situation outside briefly, he nodded in agreement until she said, "The problem is up there." She waved at the opening. "I've got Dulcin tied up and I can't get him down."

"Dulcin?" His muscles clenched. "That bastard?"

"Ackbarr and Cassai need him alive. He needs to answer for what he's done. Help me get him down and I'll drag him out. If you can take Aurin…"

"That's Aurin? I didn't recognise him with the blond hair, he'd come here with Dulcin sometimes." Mika swore internally, she didn't know what people knew about Aurin and what they thought of him here and she didn't think she could get them both out on her own. He continued, "Whatever his face said, he always smelt upset." He looked at her and waved at the cages, "We all knew and never said anything."

Mika relaxed and said, "Will you help?"

He nodded, "I'll help Aurin. You'll have to take the bastard, I won't help you with him but I won't interfere either. It'll be good to see the bastard squirm on someone else's pin for once. You promise Ackbarr will do that?"

"Yes." She relaxed, she'd have no help with Dulcin but at least someone could carry Aurin.

"I'm Carin by the way." He did help her drag Dulcin down after watching her struggle. She rolled the tall man over to check on him.

"His back's a mess, Stafa was pulling him like prey."

"Good." Carin didn't care, he went to Aurin and started looking him over. Mika couldn't let Dulcin get too battered whatever she thought of him, she needed him to be in one piece for Rufus. She went into the laboratory and found a sheet covering a cage. When she came back, she noticed that the small cat was pressing itself against Stafa, it must have decided he was safe. She tied the sheet around Dulcin. It might help him slide easier as well as protecting him from the floor. His eyelids were beginning to flutter.

Carin slung Aurin over his shoulder, staggering a bit. "Lead on then."

"Can you follow Jehanne's trail and lead us out Stafa?" The little cat spat at her words and hung back as Stafa moved. Patiently he turned and grasped it by the scruff of its neck and pulled it along until it decided to stop resisting. Mika grasped the whip and dragged Dulcin. He twisted making it harder and she kept going, ignoring the fact that he'd rolled onto his front. She decided he'd realise quickly enough that it was going to hurt far more if he didn't co-operate.

The corridor felt like it went on forever, Dulcin was heavy and Mika's shoulders were soon burning. Carin plodded on in front with Aurin dangling, following the two cats. There was more rumbling from underneath them and this time the rock around them began to shake. They all crouched, expecting the worst and got a patter of dust for their fears. Dulcin rolled, trying to get to his feet. Mika heaved, pulling him off balance and dragged him again, ignoring his swearing.

Carin said, "My memory may be dodgy but I think we're close to the top of the cliff, there are windows to the outside."

"Can we get out of them?"

He shook his head, "They're too small, although your soldiers might be able to widen them to let us out if they hear us shouting."

"Stafa's still taking us towards them, so Jehanne must have come this way." Another rumble made them both speed up as much as they could. A damp smell rushed towards them and Mika shuddered. The engineers had destroyed the ancient flood barriers and now the water was destroying the fortress that nobody else could storm.

"You're going to die in here." Dulcin's first words since he'd lost consciousness came out clearly.

"Shut up," Mika muttered. "Your view doesn't count anymore and I'm not letting you get out of dying so we can do something good for Cassai."

Carin snorted in laughter up ahead at her response and kept going. Dulcin's mutterings increased and Mika had to remind herself she was Medici, kicking him was counter to her teachings. She wished he would shut up or at least stop moving while she was trying to drag him. Aurin looked dead to the world as he bobbed up and down on Carin's shoulder. Her own shoulders ached, the whip was digging into her wrists and sweat ran down her face. She couldn't stop to wipe it off, Dulcin would take advantage of her pausing. Why hadn't she tied up his feet? Mika heard Stafa growl up ahead and swore. What now?

"Mika?" Carin sounded worried, "There are people up ahead." She looked up and saw him at a bend in the corridor, figures were coming with torches, led by a large cat.

"They're Ackbarr. We're fine." Her grip loosened on the whip in relief. It slid out of her hand too fast as Dulcin rolled to his feet and began to run. She jerked her hand away hissing at the pain. She shouted, her voice cracking, "Get him. It's Dulcin."

She was too exhausted to do anything than stagger in the general direction. A stocky figure pounded past her, racing after the tall man and tackled him to the floor. She watched in tired admiration as a swift clip to the head was administered and Dulcin folded. Another rumble shook the corridors.

"We need to leave, we've made an exit through one of the windows." Another soldier offered her a shoulder to lean on that she refused. The little cat was pressed against Stafa's side as he snarled at the other cat looking at him. He refused to move until Stafa insisted.

A large gouge had been hacked out of the corridor wall around what must have been a window. The soldier carrying Aurin neatly turned around and climbed out and down a ladder. The ladders were tied between the stone trees and carvings on the cliff face, she tried not to notice that several were starting to crack and the ladders bend.

"How do we get the cats down?"

"They should be able to jump." The Cassin who'd been leading them had changed. He grinned at Carin's stare. "You're Cassin." Carin shook his head and the other man laughed, "You'll find out soon enough." He disappeared through the gap and Carin looked at Mika, confused.

"All the royal family are Cassin." She ruffled her own dark blonde hair. "It's why we have the ability to change. We have more down in the camp, talk to them when we get there." He nodded thoughtfully and started climbing down.

The little cat stood stock still, she could see its muscles straining against its desperation not to go anywhere near the other people. Its nose was quivering at the fresh air. She tried talking to it softly, "It's good out there, you've just got to get down the cliff."

To her surprise it needed little encouragement from Stafa to jump out into the gap, its eyes wide. The larger cat jumped out with it and they began making their way down, jumping from branch to stone branch.

Mika's legs nearly gave way once she reached on the soil. Every muscles ached. She watched the two cats making their way down the cliff and wished for the chance to sleep. She sighed, she needed to start checking Aurin over. She didn't get the chance.

"Leave your pets there."

Her arm was grasped and a large soldier had hold of her. It took several minutes for her to realise it was Rufus, he pulled her into a clearing and ordered everyone away with a snarl. Mika dropped against a tree, it held her up.

He slammed a hand hard onto the bark close to her face. Before she realised, the cat inside reacted and she had hold of his throat. He swore loudly, her arm had changed completely with thick claws and fur coming out of her sleeve. She panted, trying to stop the cat from changing her further. It was yowling inside and she was exhausted. Slowly she pulled it back, forcing herself to change.

"I don't hit women, you know that." Rufus' voice was low and rough, "But I've damn well came close after that stunt you pulled."

"I'm sorry."

"You are one of my fucking subjects. I don't like second guessing what people are doing." This wasn't Rufus speaking, this was the Duke of War. "I had to pretend I knew what was happening."

"I am Medici my Lord." Mika raised her chin, she had the right to counter any order although in practise it rarely happened. Her voice shook, she'd never had to use her status like this with her friend. "Besides, Jehanne and I got Dulcin and the children out."

"And that's the only reason why you're alive. I was going to leave you to die in there until Jehanne appeared with the children." The large man had pulled away to pace the clearing, slamming one hand into the other. "The family were so pathetically grateful to get their estranged offspring back that I sent soldiers and a Cassin in to follow Jehanne's trail and find you. Being the fucking stubborn idiot you are, I guessed you'd find Dulcin." He huffed, "I know you're good with that rapier of yours but…" He refused to finish the sentence, showing the worry under his anger.

"Thank you." Mika's voice was small.

Rufus stopped pacing and in his lightening quick way, his mood changed. He swept her close, "Don't ever fucking do that again."

Being held by a man nearly undid Mika in her exhausted state. Briefly she sank her head onto his wide shoulder, smelling sweat and hot leather and pulled herself together. His hands tightened slightly and let her go with a mischievous gleam in his eye - an invitation for more. The cat caught the shadow of his long eyelashes, the dirt emphasising the creases in his face. He'd flirted with her all through the years he'd known she was a woman, she knew Rufus was intrigued by the idea of her pretending to be a man and wanted to know what she was like underneath her robes. She'd always refused to acknowledge it but here, alone with him, he was very attractive.

Mika sank back to lean against the tree behind and looked away, raising her guard again. Part of her wanted nothing more than to take up that invitation and to hell with the consequences, but she couldn't compartmentalise that part of her life as well. She wouldn't be able to look Keira or Jon in the eye again.

"No Rufus."

He grinned, shrugging off the refusal gracefully. "I thought you couldn't change?"

She collected herself. "I've not changed that much for years. Maybe it's something to do with coming back here." She tried to ignore the cat asking nicely inside. Having got out of the dank tunnels and away from Dulcin, it wanted to come out to stalk the forests. She could almost feel it rotating her ears to catch the sounds of small creatures begging to be pounced on and played with…

"Your eyes changed like Jehanne's just then." Rufus was still standing very close and he was studying her carefully.

She flushed, feeling uncomfortable under his regard. "I told you, I don't have long either."

"How human will you be inside the cat's body?"

"It's not like that, once you change completely, you may feel a loyalty to certain people but that's it, you're no longer human. It's like now, the cat may be aware of things happening but it can't influence anything." She shrugged, unable to explain any further.

"My Lord, I would ask that the Medici Mikon comes to see Aurin. I don't believe he has long." They both jumped at Jon's voice. Rufus looked irritable and Mika flushed slightly despite not having a need to.

“Jon, I hadn’t realised you were back.” Mika extracted herself, bowing to Rufus and hurried towards Jon.

He flicked a look at Rufus, “So I see.”

“You said Aurin hasn’t long.” Guilt rose - she’d not been there to look at his back in the daylight.

Jon’s voice lost its edge and became professional, “His back suppurating, I’m amazed he’s survived this long.”

“Where is he? I need to see him.”

Jon showed her to another small clearing. Aurin was lying on his side under a light blanket. He looked very still and very pale. Mika was conscious of the men close by, the low mutter of conversation overlaying the sounds of the forest. So many people in such a small space and soon they would be gone. Rufus would use Dulcin for his own political gains in Dunbarin and the game would begin again. She knelt beside the still figure trying not to panic.

Aurin’s breath was coming fast and light, Mika could see the pain in his face. “Can’t you give him sweetroot?”

“Not enough to make a difference. I’ve made this for him.” Jon held out a small cup, the brown herbs inside almost melting in the tiny amount of liquid.

Mika caught the smell, “No.”

“We can’t give him anything else.” Jon lowered his voice, “It’s not fair Mika, he’s suffering.”

She almost began to say it wasn’t fair when the memory of Varian hit her and she could almost feel his contempt for the way she was behaving. What would he have done? She controlled herself and allowed the Medici side of her to assess him.

His back was smelling badly as she lifted the blanket, it had grown worse and she'd got used to it while she'd been carrying him. It was puffy and tender, she didn't bother touching. His skin was cool and clammy elsewhere and he didn't respond to her hand on his forehead, lost in his own world of pain.

"No chance," she whispered.

"Shall I?" Jon offered the cup.

"No." She took it, she couldn't let anyone else do this. "Help me roll him over." Jon helped her prop Aurin up in her lap so she could dribble the liquid into his mouth one drop at a time. He didn't even register the movement. How many times had she done this over the last few years? She gently massaged his throat and slowly he swallowed each drop.

Mika found herself watching each breath, holding herself tightly and almost wishing that the drug wouldn't work, that he'd pick himself up and smile and laugh. Those times when he'd kissed her, taken her in his arms. Her eyesight was blurring, she couldn't let herself miss a breath, she wiped her eyes with her sleeve and she heard the sigh as he stopped breathing.

"No…" She hadn't been ready, her fingers frantically brushed at his neck trying to find a pulse.

"He's gone Mika." Jon's hands were trying to take the cup from hers, trying to calm her.

"I can't…" All thought of Varian disappeared - this was Aurin. Part of her was aware of standing up, spilling him from her lap to lie in a heap. She had to get away, the cat was offering, stretching out to take control and she couldn't let that happen either. Unable to cope she ran, leaving Jon with Aurin's body.

Chapter 17

Mika ran through crowded clearings and into the deeper forest, only knowing she had to be alone. She staggered on until exhaustion hit and leant against a tree, panting, still seeing Aurin's face, white and centred on his suffering. Her knees gave way and she curled up between the tree roots. From the first sight, there'd been something that had called her to Aurin, despite sometimes her hating him for what he was. Had it been simply that he was the first man in her own country that had smiled at her? The fact that his grandmother had been Cassin? She closed her eyes and cried for him.

She didn't know how long she'd been there, the shadows were lengthening and dark when she finally stopped. Mika forced herself to breathe, wiping her face and nose with her sleeve. The forest called around her and the cat pleaded to be let out. She wanted nothing more than to find out if she could change fully again and the fear lurked - what if she couldn't change back? She had so little time left as human, she couldn't risk it.

A noise in the bushes and alarm calls rang out. Mika swore - she didn't even have her rapier – it was back in Dubari where she'd dropped it. Stafa pushed his way through and turned to chirrup behind him. There was a spitting from the bushes and Mika nearly laughed, the sound coming out as a gasp. The little cat wouldn't come out with a protest. She wondered how long it had been a cat and if there was any chance of it changing back. Out of a weary curiosity, she began singing an old lullaby. It was one her parents had sung to all the children when they were small and she'd done the same for those few weeks with her own babies through long nights of trying to feed them, loving them so desperately before she'd given them up.

There was a nose showing, resting on a pair of paws by the time she'd finished and she started again, her voice coming out cracked, the cradle song soothing her as much as the youngster. Slowly the little cat crept out, staying in the shadows, his ears pricked and eyes wide. Exhaustion was beating its way through her, she stopped singing and just started talking gently about her own children, telling him about how she'd met them in the mountains and then rambling about Tamar cuddling up to her during their nights out there.

He stayed, his eyes fixed on her. He was very young, her two boys had been in the process of losing their spots by the time they'd changed. His fur was still full of baby fluff although his legs were growing longer in adolescence. Her fingers itched to lose themselves in the softness, to smooth the fur down and ruffle it back up again.

Stafa lost patience, the little cat squawked as he grasped it by the back of its neck and dumped it down beside Mika. He leant on it, refusing to let it spring away. Mika started singing softly again and it froze. Stafa sprawled out and having wedged the smaller cat between them and it leant against him as he began licking it.

She could feel how it trembled, she lightly put a hand on the little cat's neck and it flinched. Stafa placed a heavy paw on its back, making it stay. His licking became rougher. Mika gently began stroking the fuzzy pelt in time with Stafa, lightly at first and then harder, matching him so that the youngster was pushed first to one side and then the other. Unable to resist, its eyes began to close under the pummelling, its muscles relaxing. She ended up with its head in her lap, asleep.

It was fully dark now, the sounds of wildlife muted although she could still hear the soldiers in the distance. She was trapped under the cat and didn't want to move. Stafa stopped his grooming and huffed, snorting air out through his nostrils. Mika slowly felt herself drifting off and let herself sleep.

She woke with a tickling on her hand, half asleep she twitched and felt the warm lump at her side leap away. It was early morning, a light dew covered everything and the noise of the birds in the trees was deafening. Stafa was nowhere to be seen. Mika blinked and saw the small cat on the other side of the clearing, staring at her. He wasn't snarling, just crouched and ready to spring away again. She had a cold spot where he'd been sleeping.

Mika patted the ground in the hope he'd come nearer and he went lower to the floor at her movement. She touched her hand, he must have been sniffing at it – that was a good sign. An idea caught her and she peeled a slender branch from one of the leafy bushes. She remembered doing this with the little house cats when she'd been a child. Maybe he'd like it as well. Mika gently twitched the switch across the ground and stifled a laugh when his backside came up and his eyes widened further. She teased him as he jumped, making him chase the branch until he dropped.

He was close to her now and she held out a hand. She could see how he tensed and then stretched out to sniff. Mika lifted a finger and brushed the underside of his chin. Wide eyed, he let her and slowly crept closer. She softly talked to him about nothing in particular and slowly moved her hand to rub the side of his face and then behind his ear. He began to lean into her hand, his eyes watching her every movement. Mika kept hers averted, not wanting to spook him.

"It's good that you are teaching him to trust." Mika jumped and the little cat skittered over to the other side of the clearing. Jehanne pushed her way through the bushes.

"Will he change back?"

"Maybe," Jehanne replied. "However he may not with what he's been through. You teaching him to trust again is a start, otherwise his human side will be forever yearning for a connection it can't make."

Jehanne's eyes were diffused. Mika shivered, she didn't want to lose herself like that. Reluctantly she reinforced the iron bars she'd set around her soul. "Carin said they were tested to see if they would change."

"Some of the older Grengag in the royal family bear heavy scars, they wear them with pride to prove that they won't ever change. The tests are brutal, starting from an early age."

"It needs to stop. Both the tests and the Cassin excluding any non-changers. You all have to live together."

Jehanne dropped her head, "I will see my people safe."

"Yes, but you may have to make compromises."

Another rustling interrupted them as Stafa came into the clearing with a dead rabbit in his mouth. The small cat rushed up, squeaking in excitement and he dropped it onto the ground. Stafa lay and watched as the smaller cat pounced and hesitantly began to wrestle with it, not appearing to be sure what to do. The larger cat slapped a paw down and showed him how to gut the creature.

Mika voiced something that had been puzzling her since she'd seen the youngster, "Jehanne, Selene said that Stafa was likely to be the product of a Cassin and a cat mating but could he be a Cassin who didn't change back from an early age?"

"He could be." Jehanne studied Stafa, "He's certainly stubborn enough but it's unlikely seeing as he didn't respond to the drugs Dulcin was using in the tunnels. You said he was from the menagerie at Ackbarr?"

"Yes. Dulcin said he'd sent him there after taking his eye out." Mika didn't mention his castration.

"It would be like Dulcin to send a human born cat into a cage where he had no chance of changing back." Jehanne shrugged, "But to be honest it doesn't make much of a difference now. I can sense little humanity about him apart from the sheer force of character. He is what he is."

That acceptance again. The little cat was face deep in blood as it snarled through the rabbit, filling its stomach. What torture could make a person retreat into another form and never change back? Her thoughts turned back to her brother, for him it had been survival and then Jace dominating him as alpha.

"He's made a right mess of that," Jehanne laughed and pointed. He began to clean himself as the dawn chorus faded and the sky brightened, his stomach bulging.

Mika sighed and hauled herself up, "I need to get back." She felt a vague guilt about running away, mostly in the knowledge that she'd left Jon to deal with Aurin's dead body. The soldiers and Cassai who had died fighting had been cremated with green wood as soon as Dunbarin had been reported as taken. Cassai didn't have deep enough soil to bury bodies, especially in the forests and with both weather and animals, no body could be left for long. The pyres had been carefully sited so not to blow smoke into the camps and yet the smell had hung over the forest, reminding them all of their mortality.

There was an air of excitement when Mika got back, soldiers were packing up with no mind to be quiet. When she was seen, she was buffeted by backslaps and hailed.

"You're quite the man of the moment." Jon had appeared by her side, his voice didn't match his words and she winced. "Producing Dulcin has given Rufus the edge he needed. With the royal family surrendering this side and Dubari destroyed, Koren has managed to persuade the Cassai army officers to stand down. The Cassai army is leaking men, it's autumn and they want to get back to their compounds to sort the crops out."

"How is the feeling towards Ackbarr invading?"

"They're not happy but Dulcin was known to be a tyrant in certain circles. Information is being spread about how bad he actually was and certain organisations are being disbanded. Cassai aren't stupid, they're just concerned about what's going to happen next."

"It's not going to be easy."

"It's going to take a light touch. I was impressed by your father, I've never seen him at work before." Jon chuckled briefly, "The officers didn't have a chance. He insisted on talking to the men who'd been conscripted as well as the officers and made the men he'd brought with him do the same. Everyone knows what has happened and they'll take that information back home."

"Is he okay?" Another guilt that she'd not asked about her father, absorbed in her own problems.

"He's just exhausted. I've made him sleep and eat, he'd have kept going otherwise." He shifted, "He kept referring to me as Lin's son as well as being Medici, it felt odd. It's not something I've been ready to claim openly, even after all this time."

She could understand his discomfort. "A lot of Cassai have heard of Belindros the Medici even if they haven't met him. It sounds like he was using everything he had."

Jon shrugged it off, "We need to pack, Rufus wants everyone in Dunbarin or at least on the outskirts as soon as possible."

"Jon, I'm sorry about last night. I couldn't cope…"

He nodded, turning away slightly to stare at the forest. "I know, I just wish you could trust me." His shoulders were tense, he'd still not entirely forgiven her. "I sorted Aurin out, he was put on the pyre last night. We couldn't wait."

No chance to say goodbye. She could go to the pyre and imagine his spirit wafting up with the to become one with the trees and the sky, the ashes of his body melding in with the earth and shook her head. As the cat would say, dead was dead. She could feel its disinterest, it wanted to explore the forests of her youth, to get away from the noisy humans who were scaring away the wildlife. She couldn't, she braced herself against it and simply said, "Thank you."

"Mikon." Rufus strode into the clearing, acknowledging the delighted soldiers' comments with a wave of his hand. Jon nodded curtly and left, muttering something about packing.

"I gather we're moving back to Dunbarin." Mika was too aware of their last meeting, he appeared oblivious, concentrating on the here and now.

"Yes, I need you to be around to keep an eye on Jehanne. She's getting restless."

"She will be, she's not got much time left Rufus. She can only concentrate on one thing and it needs to be sorted soon."

He disregarded her concerns, "Koren will be coming with us, I need to consult with him over how to proceed. Cassai appear to get prickly over technicalities. Both you and Jon can help with the wounded, I'd like you to take your time travelling, I don't want your pet trying to find you in Dunbarin and causing panic." He eyeballed Stafa as he walked in with his smaller shadow. "You've got two now, are you collecting them?"

Mika narrowed her eyes and ignored his jibe - he was planning something. "You'll be executing Dulcin?"

"Yes but the details need to be right. I'll see you there." He walked off before she could say any more.

"Arses," she muttered. She wanted to be in the forefront of what was happening but she couldn't risk disobeying Rufus openly after sneaking into Dubari behind his back.

Mika found the wounded in good hands when she went to check them over. Most of their wounded had died due to the poisoned bolts shot by the Cassai. Those with less terminal sword wounds were being treated by the Cassai healers. They eyed her up as she spoke to them, both the Ackbarr soldiers who didn't know her and Cassai assuming she was simply royal family until she put them right. She lost herself in her work, enjoying the pleasure of helping those in pain and exchanging information and techniques. Jon was equally absorbed, she noticed how his comments and actions were so similar to Lin's that she had to blink not to think it was a younger version working close by.

The main parts of both armies were leaving, Ackbarr to Dunbarin and the Cassai splitting so the men could help with harvesting. She'd seen the cage with Dulcin inside go by, guarded by Cassin. Rufus would take no chances of him being freed. Dulcin ignored everyone and she was reminded of Stafa back in Ackbarr. The man under her hands groaned, taking her attention back to where it was needed.

Mika sat with Jon in a quiet area later, having washed her hands and slicked back her hair. "You reminded me of Lin so much while you were working. I'm not sure how he would have felt about all this." She waved her hand at the water still pouring out of the entrance to the keep. There was still the occasional rumble as more levels fell, she wondered when it would stop and how much would be left at the end of it.

"I think he would have tried to make sure as few were harmed and as much saved as possible. He loved this country and the people."

"I think he was more fascinated by it. The best Medici are nosy bastards." They shared a laugh.

"You said I looked like Lin but you remind me of Varian." At her look, he qualified, "No nonsense, you don't let anything go by when you're working. I swear if someone did something behind your back incorrectly, you'd have noticed and put them right."

"He's still there you know, pushing me on. He swore he'd never let me be less than I am." She hesitated, trying to work out her feelings about the sharp faced old man that she'd hated for so long as an adolescent. "Lin taught me for the sheer joy of it and I lapped it up, caught in what he loved doing. Varian tempered me into something else and I let him down yesterday."

"Varian held himself and those he thought capable to the highest ideals possible, that's why my father thought he was an arse. Lin understood that people are human, that we make mistakes and learn from them. Varian didn't tolerate mistakes."

"You said my father."

He shrugged, "Yes, I think it's time I started to acknowledge him as such. Unlike him I've never studied outside Ackbarr, this has been an experience."

"That's one way of putting it but why didn't you? You had the opportunities,"

Jon turned to her and she had to duck her head at the look in his eyes. "You know why Mika." He said her real name softly so no one else could hear it.

"I never meant to hold you."

"That's why I stayed, someone had to help you look after you."

Mika flushed, she'd never expected anyone to look after her, had never wanted it. The horror of being caged in Fenin as a married woman had made its mark deeply and the cliff edge of another cage was looming in her near future.

"Come on," Jon's voice was still soft. "Let's get ourselves sorted. We can decide how to deal with your changing when it happens love." He got up and held a hand out and she took it, blinking back her tears.

Chapter 18

Mika had almost been dreading coming into Dunbarin however it was surprisingly intact although quiet. She amended her thought to quieter – Cassai had never been a vocally demonstrative people. There were few on the streets and fewer of them were women. There was a sense of being watched as they brought the wounded in and Mika was aware of how those in charge of healing were working together with no care for who was Ackbarr or Cassai. Those being healed didn't care either, all that mattered were that the hands were gentle and efficient. It was a good start she decided.

"I'd forgotten how beautiful this place was." Jon was walking next to her, staring up at the trees wrapped around the buildings. "I just wish they could do something about the roots humping up the roads." They slowed as the small cart next to them did, to minimize any jolting.

Mika nodded briefly at a Cassai man standing in a side street, his face was tense as he watched the soldiers go by. He stared first at her hair and then Jon, then his eyes flicked down to Stafa and his smaller shadow. She caught the blink of surprise and tried to ignore the twist inside. She was considered one of the elite at first glance until they saw the cats. The Cassin would take a little longer to be integrated, the ability to change into an animal was not an easy one to stomach.

Jehanne was walking in front in a dream, her head swinging from side to side, taking everything in with a wariness and stepping lightly as though ready to bolt. This was all new to her. Mika frequently found her staring into the forest with a look of longing on her face. She'd spoken to Jehanne quietly, urging her to change and she'd always shake her head, she had one last thing to see – Dulcin's death. Mika knew that desperation, her own cat had been pleading to take her away from the smell of death and of wounded soldiers and into the clean green of the forest. Even now it was twitching inside, taking in every movement. It hadn't taken over her body in the night yet, it was waiting for something as well, some trigger point only it was aware of. She shivered, hoping it would be sensible and knowing it would only do as it wanted.

The scars of battle became more obvious as they moved deeper into Dunbarin and closer to the harbour. She could smell the sea and hear the cry of sea birds on the light breeze. The carved buildings had workmen on them, she noticed several of them had the darker skin and hair of Ackbarr. Rufus would have insisted that his engineers and soldiers helped repairs. Everyone would be aware of how most cities could be sacked, the implicit threat hung over the population and made them behave.

They began settling the wounded into the various buildings commandeered, most of the soldiers had been put into camps on the shoreline. The request came from Rufus to see him almost as soon as Mika had started to look for a place to sit. She sighed and followed the directions given. Jon joined her as she walked out into the autumnal evening.

They found Rufus in a building next to the sea front and he told them they were staying with him. A room was shown to them and she leaned out of the window to look at the sea front, seeing the Ackbarr ships in the harbour. Soon the winter storms would set in, stopping any trade and cutting the small country off via the sea as well as the mountains.

“Do you think Rufus will manage to keep a handle on things here?”

“I don’t know, we aren’t the same as Ackbarr or Fenin.”

“Most people are the same underneath, look how quickly your countrymen disappeared off to work their fields.”

“Maybe…” She wasn’t sure how easily Cassai would accept an Ackbarr yoke after being independent for so long.

“They know it could have been a lot worse, it’s been near damned bloodless for the majority of the country. The blocking of the ports and mountains have hit them hard, the common people have realised that they’re not as self-sufficient as they’d like to be. I’ve been talking to the Cassai healers, some of them are already saying they disagreed with the policies set, that they’ve heard about the various libraries and new ways of learning. Some of the younger ones are even asking about travelling to Ackbarr to learn from the Medici and you can bet Rufus and Keira will have all the traders lined up to come in and show off their wares. They won’t have a chance, your people will be fine.”

She smiled, “Let’s hope so.”

Mika and Jon stood waiting for the gangplank to be brought down from the ship tied to the docks. She could see Jon twitching at the seams of his new green robes, they weren’t quite fitting properly. Hers fitted better, she tucked her hands inside the wide sleeves, thinking they looked bare without the ornate embroidery she was used to.

The crowd had been selected, high ranking Cassai officials, officers and Cassin and any not sworn had been carefully patted down. Rufus stood in front of his officers, his scarred leather armour buffed and a rich deep red cloak over his shoulders. He looked every inch a Duke of War. Mika herself had been given a wide berth due to the cats sprawled, yawning at her feet. She wondered who was on the ship.

The wide gangplank was finally let down and soldiers marched off to stand to the side. They were relaxed as another couple of figures appeared. Mika perked up, this looked more interesting than she'd thought it would be. No one could doubt who it was limping off the ship, his arm holding a small girl - Tamar's features echoed his brothers standing on the quayside and the green robes proclaimed his Medici status.

A murmur ran through the crowd which intensified as Selene stepped off behind him. She had a richly coloured tunic on, a riot of embroidery covering both it and the trousers she wore. Mika guessed the outfit had been made to placate the patriarchy of Ackbarr and would have to do the same for the Cassai. The tunic wasn't long enough to call a dress and had slits up the sides to allow her to stride in her soft boots. Mika had to smile at the challenge in her eyes as she stared the crowd down.

Tamar walked up to his brother and inclined his head. Rufus grinned and said something in a low voice, Mika saw how Selene tossed her head and bit back a response. She could imagine Rufus was being rude to his little brother, enjoying the public occasion. Tamar laughed and walked over to where Mika and Jon were standing. He grinned at them and turned to face the ship, shifting Tahiri in his arms and whispering to her. Mika ignored Selene eyeballing her and the two cats.

There was a pause and the soldiers suddenly snapped to attention. A slender figure appeared on the gangplank and an officer handed the lady gracefully down to the soldier on land. As her foot touched the quayside, Rufus dropped to one knee, his head bowed and his soldiers behind did the same. Mika grinned, he certainly knew how to play the audience. She could see both the Cassai and Cassin trying to work out who the woman was.

The only item showing Keira's status was the slender gold circlet on her head, the rest of her Cassai clothing was rich but discrete. She heard those from Ackbarr telling others who Keira was and them blinking their surprise at the unassuming woman in front of them. Keira ignored the crowd, her attention on Rufus kneeling in front of her. The officer walked her over and then stepped back. She folded her hands in front of her and waited until Rufus looked up at her, his eyes flashing mischief.

"My lady, I give you Cassai." His voice carried and there was another murmur at the confirmation of her status.

Keira put out both hands for him to take and raised him up with a smile. She said nothing in return as Rufus took his place behind her and the soldiers stood to move aside and walked with them towards their accommodation.

"Well, I didn't expect that." Jon sniggered, "Don't you just love it when they play the sweet innocent ruler and her unpredictable spouse who can't be trusted." Rufus had a swagger in his step, his entire stance protective. Keira was smiling at the people watching and waving to the few younger child staring with wide eyes.

They followed, Mika beginning to yawn. "Keira turning up and in Cassai dress will certainly give people something to talk about."

"She decided to come, Rufus didn't want her too. He just wanted me and Selene." This was Tamar. "When he boarded the ship and found her, he wasn't happy." He winced, "It's a big ship but not so big you can get away with not knowing that sort of thing. They've all been plotting for hours with Koren."

Jon grinned, "I bet. Between the three of them I'm almost looking forward to seeing what they've cooked up."

"How was Ackbarr?" Mika dropped behind to walk with her half-sister.

Selene tossed her head and snorted, "Grengag - half of them stare at me as though they've never seen a woman before and the other half jump every time I speak. This lot look just as bad." She indicated the Cassai, her scorn evident.

"It made life interesting for a while at court. Selene needs to learn a little tact when challenging the younger Dukes to fights just because they've upset her. Stripping off to change and then threatening to rip their throats out isn't something they're used to."

"You couldn't have done it and besides, I only needed to do it twice before they stopped." Selene ignored Tamar's gentle rebuke and sounded satisfied with herself.

Mika exchanged glances with Jon, "I can imagine it caused a few waves." Part of her wished she could have been the same, it would have made her life a lot easier to be herself with all that confidence and no shame. She sighed and thought of Rosita making her own waves as a female Medici - so many changes in her lifetime.

Tamar rolled his eyes, "It's just as well I'm a Medici, I had to stitch them up and apologise to their fathers, it's not something they're used to. Anyway, we'd best get somewhere private so we can talk properly."

Dulcin stood in the cart as it creaked along the road to the space in front of the temple. In consultation with various officials, Rufus and Keira had decided it would be the best place to execute him. Mika had seen the gibbet that had been built on a stand, the noose swaying in the breeze. Cassai were generally law abiding, anything like this was usually dealt with out of sight. This couldn't happen with Dulcin.

His hands had been tied to a bar on the cart, he ignored the crowd as he passed them, staring into the distance as though they didn't matter. He looked unkempt despite his clothes being clean and neat, his face hidden with over a week's worth of white beard. No one trusted him enough to give him a razor to shave himself and he'd refused to allow anyone to be so close to him.

Soldiers lined the route, both Cassai, Cassin and Ackbarr. Rufus was visibly twitchy about Keira attending although she'd insisted. It had been quiet all the way, the crowd not even murmuring. Rufus, Keira and the others stood waiting as the cart creaked up in the silence. In Ackbarr the people would be passing comments, yelling, a spectacle made of such a man being executed. There would be food stalls set out along the way, taking advantage of those coming early to get a good viewpoint. Not here, the residents and soldiers of Cassai had filed slowly in to stand and watch. Mika could tell Rufus was unnerved, his eyes darting around, making note of faces.

It had taken a while to decide the right person to announce the charges against Dulcin, in the end Koren had offered. Rufus hadn't thought he'd a chance of being heard in the wide space, now he knew differently. The cart came to a stop. Dulcin was still staring into the distance as he was untied and led onto the platform. His hands were re-tied to a post. He looked a crumbling monument, his face impassive and with no emotion showing.

Koren stepped forwards holding a roll of parchment. “I am Koren, former ambassador under Dulcin. My wife was Dulcin’s grandchild, my children his great grandchildren and my life has been spent in service to Cassai. I have been re-instated by Keira, Queen of Ackbarr to uphold Cassai’s interests in the Court of Ackbarr and I have offered to read the charges against Dulcin, former head of the Cassai royal family.”

He paused as though waiting for a response. The winds stirred the trees in between the buildings, nothing else could be heard. Koren began to read. Mika hadn’t been in the discussions about what would be put into this document although she’d heard that Koren had argued for and against certain items. She had to admit the end result was watertight, a testament to her father’s skills. None of the Cassai in the square could object to anything being read out, even if they agreed with some of Dulcin’s views.

The only movement was the dipping of heads when a particular charge was read out that stung consciences. It was like an Ackbarr crowd shouting to Mika, she’d forgotten how her countrymen tended to curb their emotions in public. Only in private would they let loose and in company they trusted. The numbers of people dying over the years of sleeping sickness gave a flurry of heads. The average Cassai wouldn’t have heard much of what had happened and the number of lives lost was huge.

The accusations moved onto the Cassin and their mistreatment over the years. She could see the audience listening weren’t so sure what to make of this, the information that it was a natural part of the royal family was news to many. Both Cassin and those with the darker blond hair were being eyed up surreptitiously, none of the elite would trusted not to be Cassin after this and she guessed it would be a talking point in many households that evening.

Koren's reading faltered slightly as he got to the twisting of young minds to suit Dulcin's motives. He cleared his throat and carried on. Mika's thoughts went to Aurin and wondered if he'd be content with this show. She shifted her gaze to Dulcin, he'd stood impassively all the way through Koren's reading, if he thought anything of the charges he didn't show it.

It was the cat that caught the black streak across the crowd and her head jerked to see Dulcin pitch forward with a grunt. For a moment nothing happened, even Koren stopped reading to stare. Then both she and Jon raced towards him to find a crossbow bolt buried in his stomach.

"Rufus!"

She had no need to shout, Rufus had sprung into action racing down into the crowd, the soldiers covering Keira to protect her. Mika was aware that the silence had been broken and the people were surrounding a man.

"Mika…" She was busy trying to staunch the wound, knowing it wouldn't do much good, stomach wounds were never good news. Jon grabbed her arm and shook her, "Mika, look."

She flicked a glance towards the crowd and froze. Rufus had a tall young man kneeling in front of him, his white blond hair a mess, his face streaming with tears. His arms were being pinned to his sides although he wasn't struggling. Her lips formed his name, he was supposed to be dead, her father had said he was dead. She turned to look at her father and found him staring at Petron, his face white.

Chapter 19

Rufus' face was furious, he'd also recognised her brother. Mika's stomach clenched, the last time he'd seen her brother he'd threatened to slam him into the darkest dungeon they had. Petron had left Ackbarr and she'd heard something about him barely escaping an incident on the roads. She'd not known if it had been a coincidence or not. Rufus' knuckles were tight over his sword hilt and she wondered if she was going to see her brother executed in this square as well.

"My Lord…." Her father's voice carried across the silence.

Rufus jerked his head up, Mika could see him considering what to do. "Hold him there." Rufus ignored the fact that Petron wasn't struggling against the soldiers and walked back to the platform. His eyes were still flat. "Medici, leave the accused."

Mika's mouth dropped, Dulcin's blood was still warm on her hands, she could feel the way he panted in pain. He was dying and Rufus was telling her to stop trying to help. Touches on both her arms – Jon and Tamar, their faces grim, helped her up and they took a step back to leave Dulcin clinging onto the post his hands were still tied to.

Rufus put his hands behind his back and faced the crowd, "Carry on Ambassador. We will continue."

Koren stared and then licked his lips. The rest of the speech was read at a faster pace and yet it still took what felt like hours. Dulcin was curled into a ball of agony and Petron stared up at him as his father read, his eyes taking in every twitch. When

Koren finally finished and stepped back, Rufus took his place at the front.

"I was willing to give Dulcin a clean death." He waved a hand at the contorted figure. "This is what I have had to watch my country go through for the last three years. Men, women and children dying in front of me and those who cared for them. This is the payback from one of your own countrymen to his leader. Was that bolt poisoned?"

The question was academic, all knew that Dulcin would be dead by now if it had been. Petron shook his head, dumb.

"It will take Dulcin hours to die from this. Even with care, a wound to the stomach is difficult to deal with." He drew his sword, "I could leave him to die here as a judgement from one of you but we have learned to give mercy to those stricken over the last few years. I will give him the mercy he denied others."

The entire square was frozen and watching. He pulled Dulcin's head back and slit his throat quickly. Rufus turned to the soldiers at the bottom of the platform, "Put him back on the cart." He raised his head to the crowd. "A member of the Cassai royal family has died today, we will accord him the funeral due to his rank."

He stood at attention, his sword dripping as Dulcin was untied, placed on a plank carried to the cart and the crowd parted to let them through. Rufus motioned to his men and they swiftly lined the way back, Keira barely to be seen walking in her protective shield. Petron was picked up by his two guards and marched after them.

"Come on." Tamar hooked his arm through Mika's and waved at Jon, "I want to know what's happening next." Koren came with them, looking dazed.

When they got back to the residence, Rufus was ordering Dulcin's body to be washed and laid out for his funeral. The little cat jumped up from the shade of the tree in the courtyard and Stafa followed, yawning hugely.

Rufus caught sight of Koren and snapped, "Ambassador, I wish to see you inside." He put an arm out to bar Tamar from entering.

"Brother, you want me in there. Remember what we agreed?" Rufus muttered something under his breath and then to Mika's surprise, dropped his arm. Both she and Jon hurried in after them.

Keira was sat in a chair at the end of the room, the sun lighting her face. She was looking tired and sad. Stafa found the pool of sunshine on the floor and sprawled into it, ignoring the tension in the room. Petron was standing in the corner, still held by his guards although his hands were tied now. Jehanne and Selene were talking softly, or rather Selene was talking and Jehanne was staring into the wall. Her fingers were in constant motion, clenching into the fabric of her trousers. The way she twisted her head to look at them coming into the room didn't feel quite human. Mika's hand brushed Jon's arm and she slid her fingers down into his and gripped hard.

Rufus flung himself into the chair next to Keira. "Well?"

Koren knelt carefully in front of Rufus, "My Lord I must beg your forgiveness. I lied to you." Rufus' mouth dropped at his bald admission. "My son was caged with the Cassin, he came out with Jehanne and she let him go. He discovered I'd been released and found me. I lied to say that Dulcin had killed him to protect him. I had told him to lose himself in the forests and to start a new life elsewhere."

Keira looked irritable at Rufus taking over and spoke over him, "What have you to say about this Petron?" The guards brought him forwards. He knelt beside his father without needing to be forced. Petron looked half starved, his eyes huge in his thin face.

"My Lady." Petron coughed, his voice was croaking as though he'd not spoken for a long time. "I am sorry if you and your men were concerned for your safety. You were going to give Dulcin a clean death. I've watched him kill too many to let that happen."

"What makes you worthy to decide this?" Keira's voice was cool.

"I am a product of his twisted mind, I realise that now. I spent years in the company of him and those he trusted to do his wishes. I was a child when he brought me to Dubari, I thought the highest honour I could have was that of his approval. Nothing else mattered, he closed me off to anything else. The more something touched me, the more I fought it. It was only after you threw me out of Ackbarr and I came back that I began to investigate the anomalies in his stories."

He bowed his head, "I was stupid, I tried to challenge Dulcin with what I had found, still believing that he didn't mean what he'd done. He laughed at me and then caged me in with his creatures."

"Cassin, we are Cassin. We are not creatures." Selene snapped the name out.

"Yes, so I found out during my time with them. They'd been children like myself, tortured until they'd changed. How could I hate them? I would promise them that I'd kill him for them when he'd let me out to taunt me but I never could, he was too strong, too good a fighter." Tears began to stream down his face, “I couldn’t let him have a simple death, I couldn’t…” He squared his shoulders and said softly, “Kill me as well, my life is worthless. I’ve done what I had to do. Those children he’s killed can rest now.”

“My Lord, wouldn’t you have done the same? My son has realised how much he’d been used by Dulcin, like so many generations have been. He is simply a product of that. Please spare him.” Koren’s face was twisted.

Rufus leant forward, “Both you, Jehanne and Mika have lied and gone behind my back. You are the few people of this land that I should be trusting without question.” He had started out low, his anger evident. “I planned this campaign to have the maximum effect with the fewest lives lost on both sides and this is how I am paid.” Keira put her hand on his arm and he shook it off, getting up to stride around the room. “I can’t trust any of you. Other countries recognise Ackbarr as their ruler, the same will happen here. Any smidge of rebellion will be dealt with. Cassai can find out what being a completely subjugated country is like otherwise.”

Mika went cold, she’d never seen Rufus like this with the cold controlled anger dominating. Keira began to say something and Rufus cut her off. “No, I’m not discussing this. Other things can be negotiated, not this. Thousands of our people died because of Cassai. I am being generous, I will not shift on this.”

“You promised my daughter would rule…” Jehanne’s voice cut through. She sounded dazed.

“Fuck that, Cassai answers to me now.”

Jehanne made a sound, half a sob and half a growl, “Promised…” Mika found herself breathing lightly, the hair raising on the back of her neck. She could see the Jehanne’s eyes changing and the soft rumble behind her words. The cat was very close to coming out, she was barely sane. As though realising subconsciously, Rufus pinned Jehanne with a look and she stepped back, shifting away.

"No brother." Tamar sounded calm, "This isn't happening."

"Don't start trying to tell me how to run this fucking country. I'm putting up fucking forts all the way through this place, there's no way it's going to slide out of our hands now."

"You're wrong, I have both yours and Keira's signature on a document to say you wanted me to take over with Selene. You will let me deal with this."

Rufus began to splutter, "You don't have time for this, not with your studies. We'd agreed you should be a figurehead only."

Tamar raised his chin, "Tough shit brother mine, that's not what it says and it's time for me to take over now. I'm a Medici, healing a country should be similar to healing a person and I have had good teachers." He flashed a smile at Keira, "With your permission of course my lady."

Keira raised her chin, "I agree." Rufus' face flashed anger and she raised a hand, "No Rufus, we will speak about this later, I have made my decision. Tamar, we will have the ceremony after Dulcin's funeral has been held. Your title will be Duke of Cassai and you will be answerable only to me."

"Keira…"

"No Rufus, this is happening. No one need know the circumstances." Mika admired how she held his gaze until the large warrior dropped his.

"There will be talk of Tahiri being a half-breed, our country is not tolerant Tamar. They will not want her to rule after you." Koren's voice was soft.

"She will be everything Koren, Ackbarr and Cassin and she will be brought up as Cassai. I won't tolerate any racism, Cassai will learn."

"Selene was supposed to rule…" They'd forgotten Jehanne swaying in the corner.

"I believe it's Mika who's actually in direct line from Dulcin. If anyone should have a claim it's her. I think you'll find I'm doing you a favour Jehanne." Rufus was snarling, taking his anger out on her rather than his ruler.

Mika murmured drily, "Just as well, Tamar's a bit young for me."

Tamar flushed and the tension eased until Selene demanded, "What about what I think?"

"You can rule through Tamar and you'd better be bloody good to him otherwise I will smack your arse. No more fucking about with minor lords."

"Fuck off." The challenge came swift as a slap and was too close. Rufus slapped his hands down and started towards her.

Mika saw Keira begin to snap Rufus' name and something made her turn her head at Stafa's warning snarl. Jehanne had been mumbling to herself, ignored by everyone until the threat from Rufus to her daughter had triggered something inside, Mika saw her begin to change as though in slow motion. Rufus' sword was still on the table where he'd thrown it and Jehanne didn't go for the warrior, she went for Keira, the slender woman more vulnerable in her seat.

Jehanne changed while still dressed, her powerful legs propelling her forward into a leap that would end at Keira's throat. Mika wasn't armed, she'd left her rapier in Dubari. She had nothing to stop Jehanne but she flung herself in the lithe cat's path, catching her and pulling her into an embrace.

The shouts and screams in the room were nothing to her as they landed, knocking her breath out of her body. She had to stop Jehanne. Jaws were trying to get at her throat, her robes shredding under the onslaught of thick claws. Mika could hear someone screaming in a continuous wail at the pain. The impossibly soft fur, the tickle of whiskers and the raking of iron limbs thick with tendons. Her own cat fought to take over and use her own claws. She couldn't let it, didn't want it too, she'd never come back. She tied it up in her own pain and wrapped herself around Jehanne.

Jehanne yowled into Mika's ear and she cringed, her body giving into the wounds. Her arms let go as Jehanne twisted to fight something else. Mika could barely see as the injuries in her stomach and back made themselves known. She was pulled away and wished she could shriek her pain and found her voice caught in her throat. The noise came back in a rush with the agony. Jon had hold of her and was saying something, he sounded like Lin. Rufus was shouting about Stafa killing Jehanne and that he couldn't get close to help.

Everything was shutting down in her body's concentration on its injuries. Someone blocked out the light and she recognised Tamar as her eyesight began to fade. "Listen to me Mika, you must change. You need to heal yourself through changing, you can do this. Help me Jon." Mika wanted to stay human, she couldn't change. She was locked in her own battle now, every nerve raw, every sense awake. The cat wanted out and she wouldn't let it.

"Mika please, I can't help you if you stay like this." Jon sounded distraught. "Your wounds are too deep, you're going to die if you stay like this."

She was going to die, serenity poured through her at thought. She could feel herself letting go of this battered body, she was going to take the cat with her and die human, she no longer cared. Mika remembered the look of the first man who'd died when she'd helped Lin with surgery - he'd given up, the pain too much for him. That flash in a rabbit's eye when she swept its hind legs from under it in the chase, twisting to turn with it and the coiling of her limbs. The determination stayed with her, she was going to die human.

Jon's voice cracked as he shouted, "Stafa…"

The cold spread through her body and there was a grunt from Tamar as he was shoved aside. She smelt male cat, he shoved his face into hers and began licking her roughly. Another tongue joined his, smaller and more hesitant. Nothing else mattered apart from those two tongues. A trickling mind poured into her own, she had no strength left to deny it, concentrating on giving up.

Live, the cat inside her whispered and she tried to tell it that living as a cat wasn't what she wanted. It forced her to remember the starlit nights in the fields and woods outside Ackbarr, the joy in racing through the shadows, the splash of a paw landing in a puddle and shaking the water delicately off to place it elsewhere. The twitch of whiskers and stretching in the sunlight before deciding to fall asleep. Her will was failing her, she didn't want to do this, there was a place beckoning where it wouldn't hurt anymore. No more pain, no more tears. Darkness beckoned and the pain lessened, she could no longer remember her name.

A pair of jaws took her by the back of her neck and shook her gently and her body shifted, twisting from one shape to the other in a single shiver. The forest was calling louder than anything left in the room, shouting its wealth of secrets, suffocating the trail to the place she wanted to go.

Something was loosening the constricting clothes and taking them away. She cried out in her mind at the unfairness, she needed them to help keep her human, to hide what she was. She fought it all, helpless as a kitten against the hands and the mind twining through hers. Her only awareness was of her body and the healing it was being forced to do beyond her control.

The cat pounced while she was distracted and she had a moment of clarity when she could see everything in the room. A man's face was stricken as he stared down at her, she didn't know who he was, just that he was important. Another man was bending over the body of a female cat, there were rents in her side and blood all over the floor. Others were shouting or frozen into place. She wanted to reassure the man bending over her that she'd be okay, that everything would be alright and didn't know why.

Her body shivered again, pulling itself into a different shape, fighting the remaining clothing. Lost and without knowing who she was, she gave up the struggle against those refusing to allow her to die in peace. She couldn't fight any more, she was too tired. She reached out and gave herself to the cat.

Epilogue

"Medici?" The slim girl in the grey journeyman robes stamped her foot, "Medici, you need to deal with this, they need to hear from you."

The figure sat by the open window finally stirred, "I'll tell them in an hour in the library. Let Abran know and he'll arrange everything."

"You're getting drunk again." Rosita sounded disapproving.

Jon took another sip of the wine, under normal circumstances he'd never drink at this time in the afternoon but these weren't normal circumstances. "Not drunk yet. I'll be fine."

"You've been like this since you came back." Rosita hesitated and said, "I know you were close but…"

"Yes I know, people die and it's part of our job. My father used to say that if you stop caring then there's no point in being a Medici." He saw her struggling and asked, "What is it? Just say, I shan't be upset."

"I don't understand why you could care about him. He never gave praise to anyone, I had to earn it twice over every time. Everything had to be perfect, I could never match up to it." She lowered her voice, "And he always found a way to make me do what he wanted. I hated him at times."

"He knew."

"Knew what?"

"That you are a girl, living in a man's world. Everything you do, you will need to do twice as well as a man does to earn the same praise. He understood that."

"It's not fair."

Jon laughed. "I never heard Mikon say that, despite everything he went through. His life wasn't easy either you know."

"He was a man." Rosita's voice was bitter with a tone of finality to it. "He had it easy."

"You never knew Varian did you?" She shook her head. "Mikon always said that Varian stood behind him, even after he'd died. That it was like he was there, watching everything Mikon said or did. It spurred him on constantly to do more. I'll tell you about him sometime." Jon wrapped an arm around Rosita's shoulders, shaking her gently. "In the meantime, let go of your anger. Mikon was proud of you, he told me. He just wanted you to be the best, so others could follow."

Rosita was close to tears. "He never told me that."

"He wanted to but he never found the right time, he would have said eventually. Now, you go and talk to Abran and have the meeting arranged for in an hour."

"You'll stop drinking?"

"Shortly." Jon smiled as she left the room, Rosita was more like Mika than she knew, Lissina had chosen better than she'd known. He sat by the open window, staring out onto the plains of Ackbarr. He was on the road to getting very drunk and didn't care, tomorrow he'd take up his duties as Court Medici and in an hour he'd have to inform the Medici that Mikon of Cassai, a Medici of Ackbarr had died in action. The story had been concocted by those left in the room after her changing, knowing that she'd want her privacy respected.

He sighed and without realising spoke in a whisper, "Despite that, you were loved by many people Mika. Are you happy now? Not remembering? Deon said he'd seen you and that there wasn't much left. He thought you'd left it too late to change. Stafa is protective of you, I thought he would be. He waited for you, he must have known somehow that you'd need him."

Drinking had been the only way to numb what he felt, he'd not been able to cry since that afternoon when she'd changed under his hands with the two cats licking, pushing and shaking her. It had been so close, her injuries from Jehanne had been horrific. Her blood stained the robes still left in his bags.

"Does part of you still yearn for the human life? To heal people? You fought for so long not to be an animal. Will you ever be at rest?" Jon rested his head against the side of the window, "I'm going to tell Rosita stories about you, about your changing. The Cassai royal family isn't going to be a fucking secret any more. I'm going to tell her about your fighting your way through life, I don't want her hating you…" He paused, "But I won't tell her about you being a girl.. at least not until there are more in the Medici. You fought for so long to be accepted, I couldn't not allow you to have that. Being Cassai and a changer is battle enough." A tear rolled down his cheek unnoticed.

"I got a letter from Lissina, ironically the letter was dated two days after you'd changed. She doesn't know about you yet, I'll go and see her as soon as possible. You'd want me to do that, you wouldn't like her to hear from anyone else." Jon managed a bitter laugh, "You never did like to see her cry, you always felt it was always your fault." He took another swallow of his wine. "She's had a little girl, she called her Mika and she said that Maksim's finding it funny her swearing that she won't have another.

"Tamar and Selene are doing better than expected. Selene's behaving surprisingly well and

Tamar's charming everyone. It'll take a long time to heal the rift between Cassai, Cassin and Ackbarr but Tamar's stubborn and I know he'll do it. Apparently the war's good for business, traders are desperate to come over the new road and buy and sell goods. Tamar's absolved Petron on the conditions that he keeps to certain curfews." Jon snorted, "Petron is almost desperate to help. I don't think he expected a second chance at life."

Jon's smile faded at his choice of words and he put the cup down. He wasn't seeing the wounded body under his hands or the scarred cat that had staggered up from the pile of blood and rags, the one that had been chivvied by Stafa and the youngster out of the door. He saw a lithe creature, the soft grey fur ruffled by the wind in the mountains and mussed by a child holding onto her. The tall slender figure and the almost unconscious touch to the shorn head when she worried about her hair. The light in her green eyes when she was talking and the deadly grace in her movements when fighting with a rapier.

"I'm going to miss you Mika." Jon got up, he wasn't as drunk as Rosita had thought but the time for drinking was over. He bowed his head, his vision blurring, "Sweet dreams my love."

The End

***

www.ingramcontent.com/pod-product-compliance
Lightning Source LLC
LaVergne TN
LVHW010058170826
845678LV00012B/2163

9781838215767